A Wreath for My Sister

One unseasonally cold September night, as a snow storm covers Leek and its surrounding areas, Sharon Priest is out on the moors in a flimsy red dress and spindly high-heeled shoes. But Sharon cannot feel the cold any more . . .

Detective Inspector Joanna Piercy is also in red that night, attending the annual Legal Ball as a favour to her friend Tom. And now his senior partner, Randall Pelham, has pleaded for her help in finding his daughter Deborah, who has been missing for two years. Joanna promises to look into the matter, though the police investigation at the time found no cause for concern.

Two days later the thaw sets in and Joanna's mind turns to a far more disturbing crime. For as the snow slowly melts, Sharon's frozen body is revealed. As is the shocking injury which proves she has been murdered . . .

And as Joanna slowly pieces together an image of the killer, she realizes that this is not his first murder . . .

Priscilla Masters

A Wreath for My Sister

MACMILLAN

First published 1997 by Macmillan

an imprint of Macmillan Publishers Ltd
25 Eccleston Place, London, SW1W 9NF
and Basingstoke

Associated companies throughout the world

ISBN 0 333 65668 7

1 3 5 7 9 8 6 4 2

A CIP catalogue record for this book is available from
the British Library

Typeset by Intype London Ltd
Printed by Mackays of Chatham PLC, Chatham, Kent

Author's Note
The characters in this novel, and their actions, are imaginary.
Their names and experiences have no relation to actual people,
living or dead, except by coincidence.

This book is dedicated to friends, colleagues and patients at the J.K.P. and to Dave Sheppard, Police Surgeon. Ooops, I mean Forensic Medical Examiner. Thanks for an edifying weekend!

Chapter One

The snow became his ally.

It had come early this year – late in September – a date he had carefully planned without even hoping for the snow. But when he heard the severe weather warning read out over the radio he smiled and turned the volume up. This was good news. It would blanket her body, conceal it from prying eyes. Delay discovery. And help him.

The first tentative flake floated down as he lay her straight. It landed on her tarred eyelash and sat for a while like a spider's web before melting on her fading warmth to form a dewdrop on her cheek. He stood up and admired his handiwork. Then he frowned.

Something was missing. He glanced around, searching. But now the snow was threatening to hamper his escape route. More flakes landed like wisps of cotton wool, forming a random pattern on the plain dark dress. Then as the temperature dropped the snow grew bolder and faster, noiselessly speckling the navy night sky, causing the few travellers still using the high road to squint through their windscreens, put their wiper blades on to sweep the snow away and hurry off the moors, unaware of what lay behind the swirling snow.

Detective Inspector Joanna Piercy was attending the annual Legal Ball. And so far she was not enjoying it. In fact she was having a worse time than even she could have imagined.

Tom had asked her to come. 'Caro won't,' he had said. 'And I really ought to go but I don't want to on my own. Please, Joanna. Be my friend?' His thin face had been boyishly appealing. She would have found it difficult to turn him down.

And as Tom was her friend and always helped her when she asked a favour of him she had agreed. She'd even made the effort and bought a new dress.

He called round promptly at seven and she laughed at the unfamiliar sight of Tom dressed up in his dinner jacket, hair slicked down, glasses polished.

'I know,' he said, grinning. 'Hardly an oil painting. But everyone has to wear one. Then he noticed her dress. 'Wow.'

'Shall I take that as a compliment or a shocked expletive?' She laughed.

'I like it,' he said firmly. It was a clumsy compliment but genuinely meant.

She drove him to the hotel where the ball was being held and they arrived in good time to be announced by the Master of Ceremonies.

'Mr Thomas Fairway and Miss Joanna Piercy.'

A few people looked up and smiled as they descended the stairs to the ballroom.

At that point in the evening she had still been feeling bright. Tom was good company, funny and witty. And he could be delicately sensitive, too. There was to be dancing, excellent wine and a choice menu. The evening promised well.

They walked in and Tom immediately spotted some friends. He crossed the room and introduced her.

'Joanna . . . Richard McIlvoy, a colleague from a rival firm.' The grin on his thin face robbed the words of any enmity.

She held out her hand and Richard McIlvoy turned his attention to her with a friendly, firm handshake and a wide smile.

'Hello, Joanna.' His blue eyes were warm as he took in her appearance. 'That's some garment you're daring to wear. Rather flattering.' He cleared his throat and she shrugged her shoulders, gracefully accepting the compliment.

'I understand from Tom you're in the police force,' he continued.

She had learned that this could be the precursor to a complaint – say, an undeserved parking fine – a felony unresolved or a general criticism about rising crime figures and the failure of the police to tackle them.

But she had not given Richard McIlvoy his due.

'They do a fine job.'

She smiled, slightly taken aback, and glanced around the room. It was at that moment that she saw Matthew.

He was easy to spot, even hidden in the corner of a large room, his square shoulders unmistakable in a white dinner jacket that contrasted with the rumpled, honey-coloured hair. He and Jane were sitting alone at their table, she in a black dress, her back ramrod straight. Matthew was staring into space.

Richard McIlvoy was still speaking. She forced herself to listen but her eyes were drawn past his shoulder towards the corner.

Matthew hadn't seen her. She was filled with a sudden panic. Soon he would glance around the room – or Jane would. She felt paralyzed.

Tom noted her pale face and followed her glance. 'I didn't think Levin would be here,' he commented drily. 'Hardly his scene.' He touched her elbow gently. 'Come on, Jo,' he said. 'Let's sit down.'

She was grateful to him for his quick understanding and even more grateful that he found a small table round the corner, out of sight of Matthew and Jane.

'I'm really sorry, Jo,' he said as he handed her a drink. 'I thought it would be Legal Beagles only.'

'It doesn't matter. I have to see him some time. I can't avoid working with him occasionally. It isn't practical to spend the rest of my life avoiding him, Tom.'

He nodded. 'You stay here. I'll go and get us some of those delectable-looking snacks.'

Her lips were too cold now to melt the snow and it blew into the crevice between them, still slightly parted in her last surprise. Snow began to fill her mouth, blowing in little flurries as the wind whipped it around. It stuffed her nostrils, clogged her ears, smothered her eyes. Flakes sat on the network of hair, stiff with lacquer sprayed earlier. She hadn't wanted the wind to flatten her style because flat hair made her look older. So Christine had 'done' her hair for her when she had dropped the kids off. But neither the backcombing nor the promised rejuvenating glow of the chestnut hair rinse could put youth back into this whitening face.

During dinner they sat between a florid-faced barrister who drank too much and his determined-to-be-embarrassing wife.

'That's quite a dress, Joanna,' she said sharply. 'I always consider red such a cruel colour. So few women can wear it. I certainly wouldn't dare.'

Joanna stared. 'Well,' she said, smiling. 'I must say, it is rather fun playing the scarlet woman.'

But the woman was a quick match. 'Really?' she said sweetly.

And now Joanna was silent. She had wondered about the dress when she had bought it. The clinging, scarlet lurex was risqué. She knew that. But she had also known that her slim, strong figure, full-breasted and long-legged, the dark, thick hair and olive tone to her skin made it a dress that suited her. Yet as she had slipped it on earlier that evening she had become aware just how the dress clung to her outline. And she had wondered. Perhaps it wasn't really suitable for the ball. And now her confidence was slowly ebbing and she wished she was sitting at home, alone.

*

Her dress was red too. But not scarlet or lurex. She had not wanted to risk being thought of as a tart, or 'common'. Not on such an important first date. But red was to be the colour. So she had chosen a modest and cheap garment, a port wine dress of synthetic velvet combined with Lycra. It had cost fourteen pounds from the Pakistani shop in the market square, money she could ill afford. It was short and clung tightly to the slim figure with its tendency to a pot-belly. Three children had left their mark.

And now the dress was rucked up over her legs and quickly gathering snow.

No one to pull it straight.

Tom sensed her sudden change of mood and he stood up to make a showy bow. 'A dance?'

She was glad to move.

He brushed her cheek with his lips and whispered, 'No sense in being a wallflower, Jo. It doesn't suit you.' And his concern made her conscious she was spoiling his evening by being selfish.

'Yes,' she smiled. 'Yes – of course.' She glanced over his shoulder to see that people were watching them.

And Matthew was one of them.

Now the snowflakes were blanketing her pale shoulders, smothering the two, thin straps, as though nature wanted to wrap her against the weather. Her body was cooling quickly now . . . fingers, toes and nose were beginning to freeze.

Tom was unused to dancing and his movements were strange and jerky. In the end she wound her arms around him and laughed.

'Just do what I do, Tom,' she said and stole a swift glance over his shoulder. Others had joined Matthew's table and he was laughing loudly. She could hear him over the music and see his blonde hair, his high forehead as he threw his head back and laughed again. The sound made her feel sad and small and insignificant. Then she saw Jane Levin watching her with that cold, appraising stare and she quickly looked to another corner of the room.

'Are you all right?' Tom whispered in her ear.

She looked at him. 'I'm fine,' she said. 'Just fine.'

'You don't mind . . .?'

She knew he meant Matthew and shook her head. 'I really am all right.'

So they danced to the slow saxophone, oblivious now to others in the room until Joanna lifted her head from Tom's shoulder, peered over it and caught the eye of a man staring at her.

He was a stranger, sitting alone at an abandoned table, the other chairs pushed back, away from the debris, the half-filled wine glasses, plates holding the remains of food, bottles and crumpled serviettes. The others from his table had left. They must all be dancing or at the bar. But he wasn't.

And when next she looked in his direction he was still staring, his hands coiled round the stem of a full wine glass. But he wasn't drinking. He seemed oblivious to everything and everyone in the entire room – everyone except her – and his stare was intent, almost an appeal. She stared back.

He was elderly, large with a thick head of white hair and keen eagle eyes. He was frowning as he watched her and never once broke his gaze, even turning to stare when they danced almost directly behind him.

She touched Tom's sleeve. 'Who's that man? The one in the corner sitting on his own? He keeps staring at me.'

Tom glanced over. 'It's my senior partner,' he said. 'Randall. Randall Pelham.' He searched around the room until he picked out a short, plump woman in an ankle-length taffeta dress. 'That's his wife, Elspeth.'

She looked back at the man. He was still staring, and even from across the room she could sense a strong, dominating power.

Although he knew she had seen him watching her he didn't turn away or drop his gaze. Instead his stare intensified as though he wanted to force her to stop dancing – to cross the room and speak to him.

Tom looked puzzled. 'I wonder what he wants.'

As soon as they walked off the dance floor Randall Pelham approached them. He gave Tom a curt nod. 'Hello, Tom,' he said guardedly, and then turned to Joanna. 'I don't suppose you'd honour me with a dance?'

Puzzled, she nodded and followed him on to the dance floor.

The snow on the moors was falling thick and fast now, gradually disguising the shape of the body until it was a white mummy. The road was smothered. A car slithered towards the shape. The driver could have picked the mummy out with his headlights, but the flurry of flakes made visibility difficult. He could hardly see two yards ahead and he wasn't looking into the verge. As he reached the crest of the hill, the driver changed into second gear, moved over the brow of the hill and slipped down into the valley towards home. No more cars would pass this way until the snowplough carved its channel through the deepening drifts.

Randall Pelham wasted no time.

'I'm sorry,' he said formally. 'Perhaps I should have introduced myself properly.'

'I know who you are.'

'Ah yes,' he said, glancing at Tom. 'I understand you are in the police force.'

She nodded.

'An Inspector – did I hear?' He was a big man with strong arms, broad shoulders. She felt a sudden curiosity.

'I'm a Detective Inspector.'

He whirled her twice around the room in an ungainly waltz before speaking again.

'Would you mind telling me, then, Detective

Inspector,' he said rather breathlessly, 'what is the procedure for finding missing persons?'

She stopped in her tracks. The pretence was over and the question surprised her. He gripped her arm.

'No, please,' he said. 'Please don't tell me to make an appointment to come and see you at the station. I've plucked up courage tonight to do something I should have done long ago. Please, just tell me. What do I do?'

Joanna looked at the lines of unhappiness in his face. Deep lines – old lines.

'Why don't we sit down?' she said. 'So we can talk properly.'

He looked relieved. 'Thank you, my dear. I hoped you would say that.' He flushed. 'My wife says I'm not much of a dancer.' They walked towards an empty table and he pulled out a chair for her. 'Let me get you a drink.'

She asked him for a Coke, remembering that she had promised Tom she would drive him home. While he was gone she sneaked a glance across the room and saw Matthew, still seated at his table. He and Jane had been joined by more friends, but as she watched he turned and looked at her. She looked away without acknowledgement. Not a nod; not a wink; not a word.

Randall Pelham returned with two glasses and set them down on the table. Joanna cupped her chin in her hand. 'Now tell me,' she said, 'who is missing?'

'My daughter,' he said unhappily. 'My only daughter. My only child.'

She sat back in her seat. 'For how long?'

'Two years,' he said. 'Please, just tell me generally. What do the police do in such cases?'

'Well,' she started slowly, 'the way we tackle a missing person enquiry really depends on who is missing, and the circumstances surrounding their disappearance. Whether there's – as we call it – cause for concern. Everything hinges on that phrase. We have to gather the facts and work from there.' She stopped, not knowing whether she was telling Randall Pelham what he wanted to hear.

'You must understand,' she continued. 'Many people leave home for perfectly valid reasons and there is no cause for concern. The police couldn't possibly investigate every single missing person. There are thousands every year. It wouldn't be practical – or financially viable. So we have to single out the persons missing who give rise to concern and exclude situations such as domestic dispute, money worries, or suspicion of extra-marital affairs.'

'None of those,' he said impatiently.

'The nearest and dearest don't always know,' she said. 'The police simply don't have time to investigate every single disappearance. But we normally visit the home – look for obvious clues: missing passport, clothes, money, talk to close friends, take statements. We do try to find out all we can, and we take notes of insurance numbers, national health numbers, tax codes, credit card details. We find out whether the person has disappeared before. While we're doing that,' she continued, 'we take note of anything unusual at the house . . . signs of a struggle, things missing – wheelie bins, blankets . . . But as I told you, Mr Pelham, most people leave home for perfectly valid reasons.'

'She didn't,' he insisted. 'And would a woman leave her young child?'

'It happens.' She was fumbling a little.

He shook his head. 'Not in this case.'

'We would determine mental state,' she continued, a little needlessly. Pelham looked unconvinced.

'Would you arrest someone on suspicion?' His voice was thick with emotion. His hands around the whisky tumbler.

'Not usually purely on suspicion,' Joanna said coolly. 'We'd want a bit more. Some definite evidence. But,' she added quickly, 'we would probably do a more thorough search of a suspect's premises and car if we felt the disappearance was suspicious.'

The man nodded. 'I see.'

'But surely all this was done at the time of your daughter's disappearance? It's routine, Mr Pelham.'

He was silent, his eagle eyes fixed on hers.

'Did you let the police know you suspected someone of being involved?'

He looked away. 'No,' he said. 'I didn't. Now . . . Now I wish I had. There was someone, you see.'

Joanna stood up. 'It's always best to be frank with the police,' she said rather primly and then, more kindly, 'You really should come to the station if you want us to look into it.'

He looked downcast and she felt she hadn't helped as much as he had hoped she would.

'By the way,' she said. 'What's her name?'

'Deborah.'

Randall Pelham covered his face with his hands. 'She left her home two years ago.' He looked at Joanna, and she sensed the pain in his eyes almost as if it were her own. 'She left her little boy behind. Abandoned him.' He stopped. 'She would never have done that – if she'd been alive.'

Joanna sat down again. 'There must have been an investigation.'

'There was. They didn't find anything. She'd been out shopping in the afternoon and never came home. We knew she'd been finding things difficult, but surely . . . surely she wouldn't have abandoned her son?'

'Sometimes women do.'

'I can't believe it of her.' He fumbled in his jacket pocket and tugged out a crumpled photograph. It was of a lively-looking girl with dark curly hair and a huge smile. 'This is the picture the police used,' he said, suddenly bitter. 'They said she looked like a girl who enjoyed a good time. Does she look to you as though she liked a good time?'

'It's just a phrase,' Joanna said lamely.

'I know what it means.' He put the photograph back in his pocket.

'Randall. *Randall*.' Elspeth Pelham was standing over her husband, her hand gripping his shoulder.

He gave her a half-smile. 'Sorry,' he said. 'Sorry, my dear.'

Elspeth Pelham tightened her lips.

'This is Detective Inspector Piercy,' he fumbled.

'I know who she is.' Her eyes were hard and hostile.

Joanna turned back to the husband. 'I'm quite prepared to look into your daughter's case,' she said. 'But you'll have to come to the station and make a statement if you'd like us to pursue the matter. Think about it, Mr Pelham. But if there was a full investigation two years ago and they turned up nothing I don't hold out a lot of hope unless you can produce new evidence. Many missing persons are never found.' She met his eyes. 'I'm sorry,' she said. 'But I don't want to give you false hope.'

The man's face tightened. 'Don't you realize?' he said. 'Even false hope's better than no hope.'

She crossed the room, back to Tom.

'Well,' he said 'what was all that about?'

She glanced back at the unhappy man sitting staring into his glass. 'Did you know that his daughter disappeared two years ago?'

'No,' Tom said. Then he stopped. 'Hang on a minute – I do remember something. Something about . . .' He frowned. 'She'd recently been divorced. As I remember, her husband worked in Saudi Arabia . . . I didn't really know her. The general feeling was that she'd gone off with some bloke.'

'And left her baby son behind?'

Tom shrugged his shoulders, then grinned at her. 'Come and have another dance with me,' he urged. By the time they sat down again Matthew and Jane had disappeared.

Her body was completely covered now – a vague bump in the dim snowscape. No one would guess the lump had lately been a woman in a wine-coloured dress.

*

14

It was late when they left the dinner dance. The snow was falling in soft flakes on her hair. Tom watched her climb into the driving seat. 'Thanks,' he said. 'It's a luxury not to have to worry how much I drink.'

'My pleasure.'

He eyed her long legs as she depressed the clutch and started the car. 'It was bad luck, Levin being there.'

She nodded. 'I wouldn't have gone, Tom, if I'd known there was any risk of bumping into him – especially with Jane.'

'But you said you couldn't avoid him for ever.'

She gave a rueful smile. 'I only really work with him on murder cases. And thank God there aren't many of those.'

They were quiet as she moved the car up the road.

Tom broke the silence. 'I suppose you wish you could learn to dislike him.'

She looked at him briefly. 'Dislike Matthew?' she said, then stopped and pondered. 'No. I don't think so. I really don't. I just wish I could learn to stop loving him – at least quite so much.'

She gave him a quick glance, then touched his hand. 'But then you know all about loving the wrong person.'

The car slithered uneasily over the freshly fallen snow, gliding precariously round the corners.

She turned to Tom. 'I hope we get back all right.'

'Just drive . . .' he said, grinning.

It was late and few cars were still on the road, but as they rounded the corner in the centre of the town a white Mercedes shot past them.

Joanna gave an involuntary 'Bloody hell.'

Tom watched her with an amused look.

'Not going to report him, Jo? High-speed chase?' He was gently mocking.

She gave a wry exclamation. 'Something will catch up with him. Driving like that in these weather conditions he'll be lucky if it's just the police.'

'And you didn't even get his number,' he teased.

She took her eyes off the road for a second to look at him. 'Oh, yes I did,' she said. 'RED 36.'

The dazzle of a flashing blue light distracted her and it took a minute or two until it had overtaken her for her to realize she was being stopped.

A tall policeman wandered around to her window.

She pressed the button to lower it. 'Parry?' she said, puzzled.

'Evening, ma'am.' His tone was wooden. It was as though he didn't recognize her.

'Parry?' she said again.

'Have you had anything to drink tonight, ma'am?'

She sighed. 'What do you take me for?'

He repeated the question, in the same, zombie tone. 'Have you had anything to drink tonight, ma'am?' Then he produced a breathalyzer kit and she knew she had been set up.

'Would you mind blowing into this bag, ma'am?'

'Yes, I bloody well would,' she said, then glowered at him. 'Who put you up to this, Parry?'

He avoided her eyes. 'The bag, ma'am.'

She tapped the steering wheel, unable to look at Tom, but she could sense his amusement.

She grabbed the bag from Parry gave a quick puff into it and handed it back. 'Satisfied?'

He looked at the digital display.

'*Satisfied?*'

'Right, madam,' he said.

She put the car into gear, narrowed her eyes. 'Who put you up to this?' she asked again.

He blinked and she sighed. 'While you're bloody well at it solving vendettas amongst the police force why don't you charge after the damned Merc?'

'Sorry?'

'Never mind. Don't trouble yourself. I can guess.'

He stared back at her without a trace of humour.

She pressed the switch for the window, muttering, 'And you can forget about your bloody promotion, Parry, my boy.'

As they moved off she glared at Tom and they spoke the name together: 'Korpanski.'

Then she added, 'I might have known. He's always had a complex about the people I mix with.'

'The Nobs?' Tom laughed. 'A bit old-fashioned, isn't it.'

'Mike *is* old-fashioned – in many ways. I'll kill him in the morning.'

Tom was still laughing and after an angry pause she joined in. 'Blowing in the bag,' she said. 'Blowing in the *bag*! What a night.' She looked at Tom. 'I watch Matthew having a ball with his wife, have your senior partner request I find his long-lost daughter . . . get breathalyzed. Look at the snow. And it's only September.'

They both laughed.

She paused for a moment to concentrate on the road. 'I bet it's lying thick on the moors,' she said, peering through the space galaxy of swirling snow-flakes.

She changed gear carefully. 'I wonder where that car did come from. It was coming from the direction of the moors, but there was no snow on the roof.'

Tom yawned and leaned back in his seat. 'Stop being a nosey policeman, Joanna,' he said. 'Probably came from one of the side streets.'

'Still, no snow,' she said, thoughtfully.

The orange flash of a snowplough illuminated the car as it drove past, leaving the road clear, Moses parting the Red Sea. She accelerated and they were back at her cottage in under ten minutes.

At three a.m. the snowplough struggled along the moorland road, carving a lane into the drifts. It tossed a shoe into the pile of snow pushed from the road but did not go within six feet of her freezing body.

She parked the car outside and locked it, then turned to Tom. 'Nightcap?' she asked. 'Or have you had enough?'

He grinned. 'I can manage a small brandy,' he said, 'if you're offering.'

'Just one,' she said, 'and I'll join you. I need it. Then you're back next door where you belong.'

When they were sitting down, glasses charged, she turned to Tom. 'Tell me a bit about Deborah Pelham,' she said. 'My curiosity is aroused.'

Tom screwed up his face. 'I didn't really know her.

Only met her once. She lived abroad. Deborah Halliday was her married name.'

Joanna sipped a little brandy. 'I wonder what did happen to her.' She met Tom's eyes. 'I sometimes wonder about the long lists of missing persons we've circulated. How many of them are alive – perhaps living alternative lives – an existence away from previous family and friends. And how many of them are dead. How many lie somewhere undiscovered.'

'What a morbid fantasy,' he said, grinning. 'You know, Joanna, you'll have to change the subject or I'll be having nightmares.'

They both laughed at that, then Joanna sighed and stared at the glass in her hand.

'I thought Matthew looked happy tonight.'

Tom didn't know what to say. He shrugged and she looked at him. 'He did,' she insisted. 'You thought so.'

'I couldn't tell.'

She drained her glass and set it down on the table. 'Well, he isn't my province any more. And you, Tom, had better not forget. You promised to come to the police Christmas party.'

Tom laughed. 'Fine,' he said. 'But next time I'll drive.'

She also laughed. 'I don't think even Korpanski would breathalyse anyone the night of the Police Ball,' she said. 'He wouldn't know how big a fish he might catch. He might lose his chance of promotion.' She narrowed her eyes. 'That is – if he's still got one after tonight.'

'It's certainly been eventful.' Tom stood up and yawned. 'Thanks for coming, Jo. I appreciate it –

especially in the glamour dress . . .' A mischievous look crossed his face. 'You will be wearing it to the Police Ball?'

'Maybe.'

He kissed her cheek. 'Goodnight. I'll see myself out.'

As he disappeared through the door a few snow-flakes drifted in and landed on the mat, melting quickly in the warmth of the room.

Christine Rattle was peering out of the window at the silent whiteness.

The baby had woken up and she was cradling him in her arms. She bent and kissed the top of his soft head. 'I just hope your mum's having a good time,' she whispered. 'She deserves it. Life's been hard enough for her so far.'

She lifted the curtains and stared at the blank, black windows of the house opposite.

'Damn it, though, she's late. She must be having fun.'

Her sharp eyes noted things. Not only were the windows still black. There was no car in the drive. 'Must have gone back to his place, wherever that might be.'

The baby sucked at the rubber teat, taking the juice greedily. 'I hope your mum's back before morning,' she whispered.

'She's left me no milk. I don't know what you have, little thing, for your breakfast'.

The baby stared up at her. His eyelids began to

droop, his mouth hung open slackly. Christine sighed, peered one more time at the dead house and dropped the curtain. She could put Ryan back in his cot now.

She shivered. It was cold tonight. The first snow of a long winter ahead. But she daren't put the gas fire on, spend a fortune she didn't have.

She touched the baby's hands, feet, nose. Stone cold. But he didn't seem to notice. Plump and red-cheeked, he lay against her shoulder, his breathing deepening to a soft snore. She left the window and laid him down in his cot.

And the woman in the snow coffin grew colder.

Chapter Two

Dawn was bright and sparkling over the moor, the snow glistening purest white. It was quiet, too. The moorlanders had sense enough to stay inside. The animals took shelters; they had met this weather before and waited until the threat had passed. Motorists avoided the roads, putting off their journeys. The snow delayed everything, including discovery.

Joanna was up and feeling distinctly 'morning-afterish' when the telephone rang.

'Joanna?' It was Christine and she sounded hassled. Joanna could hear children crying in the background, and the unmistakable howl of a hungry baby.

'Joanna, I'm really sorry . . . I can't come in today. I was looking after a friend's kids, you see . . . She was going out. I thought she might be a bit late so I said leave them here. I told her I'd look after them for the night and she could pick them up in the morning.' There was a pause. 'Only she isn't back.'

'I expect she had a good time,' Joanna said idly. 'And it has been snowing.'

'I'm so mad,' Christine said. 'I did her hair for her.

Her nails, too. And she doesn't even have the decency to get back when she said she would. Three kids she's got, too. I've a bloody houseful. I'll lose some of my wages.'

Joanna told her not to worry but Christine was still apologizing. 'I'm ever so sorry to let you down. I'll be in tomorrow,' she said. 'I promise. Just leave everything. I'll do it all in the morning.'

Again Joanna told her it didn't matter. The cottage wasn't dirty. The cleaning could wait.

She looked around her home while she finished getting ready for work. The old furniture was gleaming from years of beeswax and elbow grease. Some of it had been acquired through the local auction sales, the rest inherited from an aunt. She lived alone, was reasonably civilized in her habits.

The cottage was small and needed little cleaning. She could manage without a cleaner, really, but she loved to return to the scent of polish and the feeling of the place being cared for. And Christine was a meticulous cleaner who didn't mind spending half an hour removing a grease mark, whereas Joanna quickly grew bored.

She decided against the bike, and backed her Peugeot 205 out of the garage. This was no morning for freezing fingertips and chapped knees. And she didn't want to fall off on the ice.

The children were all awake now and clamouring to go home.

Christine stared angrily across the road. She had a

good mind to dump them on the doorstep. She looked at the tear-stained faces and put some more bread in the toaster, then turned back to stare at the house. The curtains were still tightly drawn and Sharon's battered Fiesta was missing from the drive. Christine felt angry, not worried. She'd told Sharon not to be late back. Sharon knew she had work to go to. How the hell was she supposed to make a living cleaning with this lot to mind? Now she'd have to get the big ones ready for school. 'Art,' she said sharply to her eldest. 'You'll have to walk Sheila and Tarquine to school.' As he began to demur she hovered between coaxing, bribery and threats. 'You've got to take them,' she snapped. 'I can't take them – not with your Auntie Sharon's three to mind. Go on, I'll let you have a fifteen video out tonight.'

Arthur sulked. 'Big deal,' he said, then screwed up his face at her. 'Which one?'

'Oh – I don't know . . .' She had lost interest.

The baby started up, screaming for his bottle. 'Shut *up*, Ryan, will you . . .' Then she sat down on the brown settee and lit a cigarette. 'I can't cope, Shaz,' she whispered, chewing at her nail. 'I'll bloody kill you when I find you.'

The words held no pathos for her.

October was the oldest of Sharon's three children. She attended a small nursery school, mornings only. Once her three were safely packed off to school, Christine Rattle began to button up October's coat.

'Where's my mummy?' she demanded. 'She take me to school.'

24

Christine cursed but October was adamant. 'I want my mummy,' she wailed and William Priest took up the chorus.

'OK,' Christine said. 'If you don't want to you needn't go to school today.' She pulled the cushions off the sofa and put them on the floor, facing the big picture window. 'Look, you can sit here and watch for Mummy to come home. All right?'

The message even seemed to reach the baby Ryan. Solemnly the three children sat watching the street, waiting for the familiar green car to turn the corner. Ryan sucked noisily on his dummy. The other two watched, their mouths hanging open. When they saw the car they would jump up, shout . . . run to Mummy.

Christine switched on the television. Perhaps that would keep them amused. 'Any minute now,' she said brightly. 'Any minute now.'

Motorists were struggling along the main road to Buxton, tuned into the local radio station. No further snow was forecast but there was no sign of a thaw either and the roads were still bad. Some of the high roads had been closed. The DJ was discouraging motorists, asking the question, 'Is your journey really necessary?'

Some were. Passing places had been carved into the snow by the snowplough, but the wind was blowing the snow back across the road and, once stuck, a motorist needed boots, a shovel and some of the salted grit thoughtfully placed by the council workmen.

One of the motorists, well prepared for the weather, was digging only a few yards from the frozen body. He'd pulled into the side to allow a tractor to pass and when he'd tried to move, his wheels had slipped round without gripping. The tractor had turned out of view and the motorist was left alone to struggle against the spiteful wind and snow, glad his wife had insisted he wear his thickest jacket against the weather. Up here there were two different worlds. The quiet, warm, heated place inside the car, where you could be lulled into false security by the warmth of the engine. And the other – the raw blast of nature, the battle against the weather that took place the moment he opened the car door. As he dug out his wheels, the weather challenged him to a fight, whining around his ears like a banshee. He struggled, his eyes and ears filling with the blown snow and his fingers numb with cold, even through the thick gloves.

And as he dug behind the wheels he found the shoe. He bent and picked it up, laughed at its flimsy high heel with diamanté buckle. He could not have dreamed up more unsuitable foot gear for this Arctic waste. He glanced around him, wondering whether some girl had been stuck in the snow, lost her shoe, been forced to limp back to the car. He shivered in the biting wind and looked around at the white wilderness, his eyes glancing over the lumpy contours of the moors. No sign of the car now – or the girl. She must have escaped, somehow.

He stared at the shoe and frowned. It was new, quite a pretty shoe, for a small, feminine foot. It couldn't have lain in the snow for long. He wondered what to do with it. The stocking salesman grinned. If his wife found that . . .

Then he should throw it away. But it was clean and new. The tips of the heels were unworn and the toe was quite clean . . . The maker's name was still legible. The shoe had come from one of the local factory shops and must belong to a local girl. He stared at it and was aroused by it. He thought he would like to see its owner. He pictured her . . . small and slim with shapely legs and pretty feet.

She had been all of these things.

He frowned across the white expanse. What had she been doing up here? Then he thought, maybe the girl would come back and look for it. And as he held it he felt superstitiously bound to its owner. Perhaps if he kept it he would find her.

So instead of tossing it back to the snowbound land-scape he placed it very carefully in a small box in the back of his car. He didn't know what he would do with it. It was enough simply to know it was there. Then he finished digging out his back wheel, put the shovel in the boot of his car, next to the box, eased the vehicle carefully out of the snowdrift and moved out on to the road.

All the time the stocking salesman was aware of the shoe in the box.

When Joanna arrived at the station at half past nine she marched up to Korpanski's desk.

'What's the bloody game?' she demanded.

He said nothing. He was a big man, muscles

encouraged by body building, with dark eyes and jet-black hair – a reminder of his Polish ancestry.

'For goodness' sake,' she said. 'I might have been over the limit.'

'Good morning, ma'am,' he said formally.

'Don't ever try that on me again, Mike.'

He grunted.

'I mean it, Mike. It was a rotten trick.'

She paused. 'And how long had Parry been sitting outside waiting for me to come out?'

He stared straight ahead.

She took a deep breath. 'Nothing to say?'

There was no mistaking the hostility in his dark eyes when he looked up.

'So grumpy, Mike,' she flared. 'Now what's the bloody matter?'

'Nothing,' he said finally. He bent towards the computer screen and faked total absorption.

She looked around the room. One other officer busy at his work. She sat on the edge of Mike's desk. 'All right, Tarzan,' she said. 'What's the problem?'

He leaned right back in his chair and stared at her, with something very like hurt at the back of his eyes.

'Hobnobbing at the Legal Ball,' he said, looking at her.

'Mind your own business,' she said. 'It's nothing to do with you.'

His eyes gleamed. 'Have a good time?'

She nodded. 'It was all right.'

He looked at her, eyebrows raised.

'I met Tom's senior partner,' she said. 'He asked me

to look into the disappearance of his daughter. She vanished two years ago. Do you remember the case?'

'Women are always going missing,' he said, scowling. 'What was her name? I'll dig out the file.'

'Deborah. Deborah Halliday. Her maiden name was Pelham. It was roughly two years ago. She disappeared leaving a child behind – a little boy. He was only eight months old.'

She hesitated, then put her hand on his arm. 'Mike,' she said awkwardly, 'don't make things difficult for me.' She weighed up whether she could confide in him and decided against it. He would not be sympathetic. He had never liked Matthew. So she sighed and said nothing about having seen him. Instead she concentrated on the missing girl.

'Her father seemed a nice man,' she commented, 'if a trifle forceful. Still very upset at his daughter's disappearance.' She stopped. 'I'd like to help him.'

Mike said nothing.

'Please,' she said.

Mike nodded briefly and pushed past her. 'I'll get the file, then,' he said. 'I wouldn't want your legal friends disappointed.'

Her temper, already stretched by the tensions of the night before, snapped. 'Oh, for God's sake . . .'

And, unpredictable as ever, Mike grinned. 'Well,' he said. 'There's nothing much doing here this morning. Not unless you count shoplifting. I suppose we may as well open up an old case.'

She made a face. 'No, I do not count shoplifting. One of the PCs can sort that one out.'

'Don't you mean one of the WPCs?'

'Why? What's been stolen?'

He looked at his pad. 'A dress,' he said. 'A red evening dress.'

Then he grinned again. 'What did you wear last night, Inspector?'

'A red evening dress.'

'I don't think that would impress your solicitor friends.'

'What?'

'Wearing a stolen dress.'

They laughed together then, and the tension that had begun the morning was over.

Mike returned ten minutes later with a thick manila file and handed it to her.

'Did you deal with the case?' she asked.

'Yeah.'

Joanna looked up at him. Matthew had once given Korpanski the nickname of Tarzan, mocking his stolid attitude combined with extraordinarily well-developed muscles. Matthew had a keen if cruel wit, but as usual it was spot on. The nickname suited Detective Sergeant Korpanski. Prickly, sometimes quite obtuse, with a huge chip on his shoulder, but . . . She smiled. She had grown used to working with him. They were a team – even if it was sometimes an uneasy team . . .

She stopped dreaming. Mike was speaking to her:

'As Dad was something of a mouthy bigwig,' he said, 'we did a pretty fair job of hunting for Deborah.'

He produced a picture of the girl, a copy of the one Joanna had seen pulled from Randall Pelham's pocket.

'These are the facts. She left her husband in Saudi

Arabia six months before she disappeared, taking with her her baby son, Sebastian.'

Joanna gave Mike a questioning look and he nodded.

'Yes,' he said. 'You've guessed it. There was something going on in Saudi. At least there was a rumour – only rumour – but one or two of her friends said she'd had an affair out there.'

Joanna blinked.

'The penalty for adultery in Saudi Arabia is something between public stoning and fifty lashes. She scuttled back to Britain – to Daddy's influence and the slightly more lenient laws of the UK.'

Joanna sighed. 'No wonder he was a bit prickly when one of the police called her a "good time girl". Then what?'

'She'd managed to get a small council house in Leek on the Roaches Farm Estate.' Mike fingered through the file. 'She seemed to settle quite well there – had a few friends. There are a few single mums living there and they support one another, look after kids, go out together . . . She went out shopping, up to the market, that Wednesday, leaving the little boy with a friend – a woman who lived across the street. She said she was popping up the market to get some underwear and a pair of socks for Sebastian.' He grinned. 'Don't know where some of these women get their kids' names from.'

'And?'

'She never came back. No one worried until late that night. And no one called the police for two days. Everyone kept thinking she'd gone off with a bloke for a couple of days and would eventually turn up.'

He paused. 'But she didn't.'

'She abandoned the child?'

Mike nodded. 'It made us a bit suspicious, but he was a sickly kid. Thin and miserable. According to her closest friend, he cried a lot, especially in the night. I think she'd found life difficult. There was nothing particularly suspicious about her going.'

'Is there more?'

Mike nodded. 'She was more of a good time girl than her father had any idea of. There were stories of late nights and noisy parties. Two hundred pounds had been withdrawn from her building society account that afternoon, leaving it practically empty. A dress was missing from her wardrobe. It was a party dress – red. Some high heels and her bag of make-up were gone too, together with some toiletries – a toothbrush. We did all the usual enquiries, took statements. She'd been up the market that day. Bought some underwear all right, but we asked at all the stalls that sold kiddies' clothes, and she didn't buy the socks for Sebastian. Nothing for him at all. She wasn't seen after about two thirty. She'd just disappeared. There was a possible sighting on the Manchester train but it wasn't anyone who knew her. But her friend told us she'd been a couple of times to a gambling club in central Manchester. There was nothing suspicious at the house. After a couple of weeks of nothing we decided she'd met up with someone who didn't want the kid – and had hopped it—'

'But no name was forthcoming?' she interrupted.

'No. No name, but neither was any cause for concern ever unearthed.'

'Yet her father wasn't satisfied?'

Mike shook his head. 'Definitely not. They never are. He was convinced we weren't doing all we could to find out what had happened to her.' Mike's eyes met hers. 'Like a lot of fathers he simply didn't know his daughter. He kept saying she couldn't have abandoned the child.' He stopped. 'I never met Deborah but I did see the child and judging from her photograph I would say there was a high chance she wanted a good time without the kid.'

She nodded. 'Did you get anything from her friends?'

'Apart from the woman who watched her kids she only really had one close friend – Leanne Ferry.' He grinned. 'One of the spiky-haired brigade. A feminist. You know, I can never get inside the minds of some of these women.'

'I know,' she said drily.

Mike grinned, for once refusing to take offence.

'So what did this ardent feminist have to say about her missing friend?'

'Not a lot. She said she'd been lonely . . . and that the little boy had been getting on Deborah's nerves. It sort of confirmed our suspicions.'

'You didn't chase up the Saudi connection – the affair that had led to the break-up of her marriage?'

'We telephoned the husband. He couldn't help us with a name. He simply knew she'd been having an affair – anonymous letter. The usual thing – from a friend.'

'Any other friends over there? Girlfriends?'

'No help at all,' Mike said. 'And we couldn't justify

going there. She'd disappeared from here. And she certainly hadn't gone back there without the child. It all seemed like just another disappearance.'

'Just another disappearance...' She shrugged. 'Well, I'll have a read of the file. See whether anything springs to mind. Did you tell her father everything?'

'Most of it,' Mike said reluctantly. 'And he didn't like it.'

Joanna nodded.

'She was a good-looking girl.' Mike glanced down at the picture. 'You can't blame her for running away.'

'So she was filed as a missing person?'

'Yes. We never found anything, Jo.'

She paused, scanned some of the reports. They all concurred with Mike. 'What happened to the baby?'

'I think he went to live with his father,' he said.

She frowned. 'And Deborah's never been heard of again?'

'A couple of supposed sightings. Nothing conclusive. Never anyone who knew her. We kept the investigation on a back burner for six months, but nothing.' He looked at her. 'Really, Jo. Nothing. She disappeared into thin air. You know how many people do that every year. We can't keep hunting for them all.'

'Quite,' she said and picked up the sheaf of papers. 'Leave these with me. I'll read them through properly.' She crossed to the window. 'The snow's starting to melt,' she said, watching the slow drip from the opposite roof. 'I wouldn't be a bit surprised if it's gone by the end of the day.'

*

The warmth came from the sun and softened the snow. Inkblots of heath appeared and spread, growing larger each hour. And, as the snow melted, a thin, warm mist made the air damp and the view less sharp, more untidy. Drivers became bolder, assured by the local radio station that there was no chance of further snow. It was safe to travel. Shopping trips were resumed and the farmers hunted out their animals with tractors laden with silage and hay. Life got back to normal.

Except for her life.

The chill in her body prevented the snow from melting, so although the dark patches spread during the morning, even by early afternoon she lay in one of the deeper drifts, her shape still indistinct.

By the time the three children wandered home from school Christine had had enough. The baby had cried all day. She must have bought the wrong type of milk because he still seemed hungry. The last of the box of disposable nappies Sharon had left last night had been used and she had told the other two to come away from the window hours ago. There seemed no point in watching. By the time the second night fell she had almost given up hope that Sharon would come back at all. She was left with the children and she was fed up. 'I'll give it one more day,' she promised herself. 'Just one more day. Then I'm getting the Social Services in.'

At the end of the day Joanna came out of her office, found Mike and together they wandered across the road to the pub. She ordered a pint of beer and a glass of wine and they sat together and drank.

'Not your evening at the gym, Mike?'

'Not tonight.'

He eyed her over the rim of his glass. 'You didn't really mind Parry breathalysing you last night?'

She leaned forward. 'You do realize, Mike, if I *had* been over the limit he would have been forced to prosecute.'

'You wouldn't have been over the limit,' he said stoutly.

'You have such faith in my integrity? After all that's happened?'

His eyes flickered and he said nothing. But talking about the drive home last night had reminded her of something else.

'Does a white Merc, numberplate RED 36, mean anything to you?'

Mike nodded. 'Charles Haworth,' he said. 'Flash accountant. Why?'

'He passed me at speed in a blizzard last night,' Joanna said drily. 'Just before PC Parry did me the honour of treating me to the breathalyzer.'

Mike grinned. 'You fancy nabbing him?'

'Just out of pique because he drove faster than me in a blizzard? Certainly not.' Then she laughed. 'Is he easily nabbable?'

Mike shook his head. 'Not really. For his reckless driving Haworth's well known. He's had quite a few cautions. But apart from that he's clean – as far as any accountant's clean.'

She wagged her finger at him. 'Naughty, Mike. Prejudice. I think I'd like to meet this accountant.'

Mike's eyes flickered. 'Not your cup of tea,' he said. 'Not a bloody lawyer – or a doctor.'

She let herself into the cottage to the sound of the phone ringing.

It was Matthew. 'It gave me a shock last night,' he said, 'seeing you there. I'd forgotten Tom is a solicitor.'

'Did you and Jane enjoy it?' Even to her own ears she sounded formal and unnatural.

'Yes.' His voice seemed strained.

'Matthew, why did you ring?'

'I wanted to tell you . . . I thought . . .' he said. 'I thought . . .'

There was a long pause. 'You looked wonderful. I really thought you looked wonderful.'

She took the compliment coldly. 'Thank you.' And then all the closeness between them seemed to flood back. 'Actually,' she said, laughing, 'I felt a bit over-dressed.'

'Well,' and he laughed too, 'not many women would have turned up to the Legal Ball wearing a dress that wouldn't have looked out of place at the Oscar's Ceremony.'

'Oh dear,' she said. 'Was it really that bad?'

'No. Not at all. But everyone will have noticed what you wore.'

There was another pause, then Matthew said, 'Jo.' He spoke very softly. 'Please, can I see you?'

'No.'

'Darling. You can't avoid me for ever.'

'No,' she said again and dropped the phone like a hot brick.

She sat motionless for a while, in turmoil after Matthew's call. Then gradually she became aware of her surroundings again. And as she did so often when she was upset she opened the door of the glazed cabinet in the corner of the room. She had inherited the cabinet from her aunt when she was twenty-one, newly graduated from university with a psychology degree that had always been meant to lead her to a greater understanding of the criminal mind as well as a career in the police force. She knew the decision had been a disappointment to her parents, her mother bitter from the divorce, her father struggling to match his new wife in age and shed twenty years.

But the aunt had understood Joanna's career plan – and had approved, too. So her death came as a shock. And the pieces of antique furniture, together with the real treasure – a quantity of nineteenth-century Staffordshire pottery figures – she had left to Joanna were doubly precious. Sarah, her sister, called them her 'dolls' and taunted her when she found Joanna fingering them. But to Joanna they were her rogues' gallery, hardened criminals made locally in the last century when the pious Victorians had had such fascination for evil and crime. Joanna's aunt had started the collection and now whenever Joanna was free she would scour the local flea markets and salerooms as well as the antique shops for some new criminal figure.

She picked the nearest one out. Palmer the villain, Palmer the poisoner. But not even he could distract her from the welcome memory of Matthew's voice. And now she wished she had said yes.

It was a cloudy night on the moors, the temperature a little above freezing. A fine rain washed the ground, rinsing the snow off the red dress, washing her face, her legs, her hair. When the first light broke, the body would be visible from the road.

The stocking salesman smiled to himself as he remembered the shoe he had so carefully placed in the box in the boot of his car.

Chapter Three

It was a farmer, driving his tractor to reach sheep sheltering from the weather, who was the first to spot her. He peered through the morning gloom and saw a patch of red in the melting snow. Shouting to his dog, he pulled off the road, switched off the spluttering engine and crossed the field.

Joanna sat up in bed, peered out of her bedroom window and knew there was no excuse not to use her bike this morning.

It felt good to be slipping on her shorts and tracksuit, to feel the wind in her face again. And although the wind felt raw as she wheeled her bike out of the garage, she knew she would soon be warm.

She turned out on to the main road, then faced the hill climb towards the town. The hill was a challenge and she pedalled steadily in a low gear. Halfway up, she slowed and grimaced. A couple of days' laziness had their price. Her legs were aching. And so was her back.

'Come on . . . Keep going.'

She had a companion. Tall and slim with beautiful

white teeth and quick, strong legs. He slowed down to keep abreast of her. 'I've missed you the last couple of days,' he said cheerily. 'The snow put you off?'

'Just a bit,' she admitted.

'Tough getting back in the saddle.' He grinned.

Panting, she agreed.

'Name's Stuart,' he said.

'Joanna.'

They reached the top of the hill together just as a lorry thundered past.

'Work in Leek?' he shouted.

'Yes.'

'What do you do?'

A natural reluctance to divulge her profession always made her say she worked in an office. 'And you?'

'Nuts and bolts man myself.'

He glanced at her bike. 'And that's a nice bike, Joanna.'

'Thanks.'

He gave her another flash of white teeth. 'Do you live in the village cottages?'

Something stopped her then. She lived alone and usually felt quite safe. But weren't the police always warning women to be careful, to keep their addresses and telephone numbers from all but close and trusted friends? She looked at him.

'In Cheddleton.'

'Whereabouts?'

'In the village,' she said vaguely.

He took the hint. 'I see,' he said, then grinned again. 'I've noticed you lots of mornings, cycling in to work.'

'Oh.'

'I always notice a good bike,' he said, 'and a good pair of legs.'

She was silent until they reached the outskirts of the town and Joanna gestured. 'I have to turn off here.'

'I know. I've seen the way you go.'

Again Joanna felt the vague apprehension and remembered a plaque from her childhood. It had begun 'Christ is the head of this house'. But it had been the rest that she had found disturbing.

> *'The silent listener to every conversation.*
> *The unseen guest at every meal.'*

It had been the concept of an unseen watcher that had unsettled her during meal times. She felt the same apprehension now.

She had never noticed him before. And she too noticed a good bike – and a good pair of legs.

'Bye,' she said as she approached the corner.

He shouted after her. 'I'll see you tomorrow, Joanna.'

Mike was manoeuvring his car into the parking space. He watched her spin into the yard. 'I didn't think you'd bike it in today,' he said. 'Aren't you cold?'

'Not while I'm moving.' She laughed. 'But I am when I'm standing around here in the car park talking to you.'

'Rather you than me. Give me a nice warm car to get to work and a comfortable gym to get my exercise.'

'Softy,' she chuckled and chained her bike to the railings. 'I had company today.'

Mike raised his eyebrows.

'A rather persistent cyclist named Stuart.'

'Lucky you. I hope he was wearing padded shorts.'

She punched his arm lightly. 'Of course. And he was very good looking.'

The banter with Mike was one of the things she liked most about him. It made him easy and comfortable to work with – most of the time. But Mike had his sensitive spots.

The call came through at eight forty-five exactly. Instinctively both she and Mike glanced at the station clock when they heard the slow voice of the farmer.

'Don't touch anything,' she instructed. 'We'll be with you as soon as we can.'

She looked at Mike. 'Get Moorland Patrol. I want them up there as fast as they can. I want the whole area sealed off for the SOCOs and the photographer.'

Mike picked up the other phone while Joanna took directions and asked the farmer to stay where he was. Then she and Mike climbed into a squad car and turned up towards the moors.

His face was tense. 'Do you think her car broke down,' he asked, 'and she got out to walk, and then got lost in the snow?'

'Let's just wait,' she said, but in the silence they both met their own private dreads. Bodies were not pretty things and Joanna recalled a lecture she had recently attended. Most murder investigations are bungled from the outset. Ninety per cent of forensic evidence is missed from the scene of the crime.

She determined not to lose the thread.

The site was marked by both the tractor and the flashing blue light of the squad car. Joanna glanced around at the fast-melting snow and thanked God for the rise in temperature. She shivered as she contemplated the idea of a someone lying out on the moors undiscovered. Perhaps a killer walking free, with no one even aware of his crime.

PC Timmis looked grim as he walked towards the car. 'It's a young woman,' he said. He swallowed. 'I think she's been dead a couple of days.'

McBrine was taping off an area to one side of the road, and two constables were erecting a plastic tent. Joanna approached slowly.

A young woman lay, arms outstretched, under the awning. She wore a sodden red dress and her hair was an unnatural shade of chestnut and thickly teased in an elaborate style. Her long legs were clad in dark tights, and she wore one pretty black high-heeled shoe with a diamanté buckle.

And on that cold, raw day, rain dripping and melting snow trickling on the heath, she lay surrounded by stillness and the cluster of grim-faced officials.

Joanna peered at the girl. Bruises shadowed her eyes like a grotesque parody of make-up. She had been dead for a while.

'We need a major incident team,' she said quietly to Mike, 'and the forensic pathologist. I'll ring Matthew.'

The farmer was standing by to be interviewed.

'Good mornin',' he shouted as Joanna approached.

'I'm glad you found her,' she said. 'The sooner the better. I don't suppose you recognize her?'

The farmer shook his head. 'Never saw her before.' He looked at Joanna curiously. 'When do you suppose she was put there?'

'Before the snow.'

'She been there two nights, then. It started nigh on midnight, Tuesday.'

Joanna nodded. 'On Tuesday,' she said. While Tom and I were dancing someone was killing this girl and dumping her body. It was an ugly thought. She turned her attention back to the farmer. 'There won't have been much traffic that night.'

'Near enough none at all. And yesterday there weren't a lot, though the snowplough shifted the snow off the road. Town folk. They steers clear.' He gave a toothy chuckle. 'The moors frightens them so they sticks to them 'omes.'

'At what time did you find her?'

'Eight thirty. It were dark before then.' He glanced around at the empty moor. 'Gloomy sort of place, ain't it?'

She agreed. And yet it had a wild charm. Raw and cold. The moor felt challenging.

'Were you here at all on Tuesday evening?'

The farmer thought. 'Not after six,' he said. 'We stayed in.' He looked around. 'The weather were rough.

45

The snow were threatenin'. I knew the sheep would find shelter.'

'I suppose they have to?'

'Aye,' he said. 'Or they die.'

He had the matter-of-fact acceptance of life and death that she had met before here on the edge of civilization.

'Could she have been there earlier on on Tuesday evening?'

'I don't think so.' He scratched his woollen bobble hat. 'No, I'm certain she weren't. I would have noticed it for sure. Anything different.' He glanced around. 'You see, I know these moors well.'

Joanna nodded. It was true. These people did know every inch of this wild, wind-blasted place.

So the body had almost certainly been dumped after six p.m. on Tuesday night but before the snow fell heavily. Joanna thought for a moment. The snow always reached the high ground first. It had been nearly two a.m. when she and Tom had driven home. So that made it after six p.m. and before two a.m., when the snow was too thick for traffic to pass. As far as she had been able to see, there had been no snow underneath the girl.

She looked back along the road. The bright head-lights of the maroon BMW announced Matthew's arrival. He had wasted no time.

She walked to his car and opened the door. 'Hello,' she said.

His eyes warmed as he looked at her and he smiled. 'I told you you wouldn't be able to avoid me completely. I just didn't think it would be so soon. What have you got for me?'

'A young woman,' she said. 'All done up for a night out. Matthew . . . I think she's been strangled.'

He nodded, took his case out of the boot.

Mike was walking towards them. 'Photographer's here,' he said, giving Matthew the briefest of nods, which was scarcely returned.

The three of them picked their way along the narrow, taped corridor which led to the body. Timmis and McBrine had cleared the path.

Matthew pulled on surgeon's gloves and knelt down by the girl. 'The rectal temp'll be a waste of time,' he said. 'It's been so cold up here. But that'll have delayed putrefaction anyway.'

She felt her usual queasiness confronted with Matthew's cheerful facts.

'Still stiff,' he said, lifting one arm. 'Probably been dead less than forty-eight hours. Very difficult to tell in these conditions.'

'From what I can work out the body was placed here before the snow fell.'

He looked up at her. 'Tuesday night?'

'I think some time after six . . . The farmer uses this road fairly regularly. He doesn't think she was here late on Tuesday afternoon.'

Matthew nodded thoughtfully. 'Tricky circumstances,' he said, 'with the snow, but I think Tuesday night's about right.'

He looked closer at the girl's neck. 'Looks like strangulation,' he said, and leaned forward to finger the dark marks. He stopped abruptly. 'God.' He turned to the photographer. 'Get a picture of this.'

'Strangled?' Joanna asked.

'Garrotted.'

'What?' Mike was frowning.

'I think it's a wire ligature,' he said, 'but so deeply embedded in the neck I can't tell until I get her to the mortuary. Look.' He moved the girl's hair away from the back of her neck to expose a piece of wood knotted into thin wire. 'Looks like a piece of broom handle.'

Mike touched Joanna's arm. 'You all right?' he asked gruffly.

She gave a weak smile.

Matthew was absorbed in his work, directing the photographer to the face, the hands, the neck, the position of the body.

'She's been neatly placed,' he said. 'Laid to rest.'

He worked steadily for half an hour before he stood up and issued instructions. 'I've finished,' he said. 'For now. Get her moved to the mortuary.'

Mike glanced at Joanna and she knew exactly what he was thinking. His dark eyes watched her with concern. Matthew's insensitivity. She closed her mind to it.

'Anything else, Mat?' she asked.

He faced her and smiled. 'You were right, Jo. She was put here just before the snow started. I think she was garrotted somewhere else – possibly in a car – probably from behind not long before she was driven here and dumped late on Tuesday night.' He started peeling his gloves off. 'I'll be able to tell you much more after the PM but it looks as though she was raped first.' He stopped and grinned, remembering her weakness. 'You *are* coming to the PM?'

Mike was clearing his throat and Matthew shot him an amused glance. 'Unless you fancy coming, Korpanski.' He paused. 'Or do they make you feel ill too?'

Mike flushed.

'Do we know who she is?' Matthew said as he headed back to the car.

Timmis was walking towards them holding a sodden black handbag.

'I think we're about to find out,' she said. 'Thanks, Timmis.'

She opened the bag. A typical woman's jumble ... keys, make-up, Tampax, red plastic purse. And a name. Joanna glanced back at the plastic tent erected over the body and at her colleagues already searching the area.

'Sharon,' she said. 'Sharon Priest.'

She spoke to Mike then. 'Forty-five Jubilee Road.' She paused. 'Can you take over here while I attend the PM?' She grimaced. 'You know what Matthew's like. He wants to do it straight away. We'll meet back at the station at lunchtime and go round to Jubilee Road this afternoon. See what we can glean.' Then she looked around at the bleak scene. 'Let's bag the rest of the stuff up.'

Mike gazed around the moor. 'I wonder where her other shoe is?' he said.

Joanna settled into the passenger seat of Matthew's car. For the first part of the journey Matthew chatted easily about the circumstances of the woman's death. Joanna half listened, her mind racing with the pleasure of being with him and with thoughts of all she had to do ... arrange a press conference ... inform relatives ... unearth suspects.

It would probably turn out to be one of those 'domestic' crimes. The woman killed by someone she already knew – a husband, a lover, a boyfriend. A jealous man. A complete stranger. A sex crime.

She became aware that Matthew had stopped talking and had turned to look at her.

'Jo ...' His voice was gentle. He was watching her with a half-smile, his green eyes warm and shining.

'What?'

He rested his hand briefly on her arm. 'Please,' he said. 'I just want the chance to talk to you.'

She looked not at him but out of the window, to the honest, damp green on the moor. 'Matthew,' she said in a calm, even voice. 'There isn't anything to talk about. We had an affair. You're married. You have a daughter.'

His eyes could turn different shades of green. She had noticed this before. Emotion changed their colour, whether it was anger or love. And sometimes it was simple lust.

'You never gave me a chance to explain anything,' he said.

She looked at him with the faintest tinge of irritation. 'What the hell is there to explain? It's the oldest story in the book. Married man meets single woman. They make sparks in bed. He goes home, which is where he belongs.' She stopped. 'Look, Matthew, I don't know whether you loved me or not. In a way it's irrelevant. You're married to Jane. Still. Please, don't insult my intelligence or integrity. I don't mind but I do like to know where I stand.'

Matthew had a habit when he was ruffled of running his fingers through his short blond hair, making it stick up. He did it now and gave a short, rueful laugh.

'You're a very determined person, Jo,' he said quietly. 'But I think you've misunderstood me completely. And that's what I want to talk about.'

They had arrived at the mortuary. She opened the car door. 'Will you ring the Coroner or shall I?'

'You can,' he said. Then he surprised her by leaning across and giving her a soft kiss on the cheek.

'What was that for?'

'For being brave.' He laughed. 'I know you hate PMs. Now come on, let's see what mysteries the morgue throws up.'

An hour later Matthew was washing his hands. 'Well,' he said. 'A nasty way of killing someone, especially after a pretty violent rape.' He stopped. 'Her underwear was removed. She was obviously dressed up. For a date, maybe. If so it was a cheap date. Despite the glamorous dress' – he indicated the sodden pile of red material the mortician had cut off the body – 'the stomach contents show a small amount of cider. Nothing more. No food. I think initially she might even have agreed to intercourse.'

'Not technically a rape, then?'

'Perhaps technically he had her consent. But he didn't have her consent to the rest. The lovemaking became increasingly violent. There was a lot of bruising. And it culminated in this.'

He fingered the wire ligature, cut carefully to preserve the length of broom handle twisted into it. 'It'll have to be sent off with all the other samples. I'll keep the knot, but I suppose you want some of the cable.'

She nodded. 'It'll be important for the investigation.'

'Of course the real prize is the semen.' He dried his hands on the hospital towel. 'Find me a suspect, Jo, and I'll prove it was him.' He stopped. 'It'll be a cut-and-dried case thanks to DNA profiling.'

'That and the rest of the evidence,' she said. 'But if only it was so easy. Unfortunately I'm already picking out the defence. 'We made love, Your Honour . . . I wasn't the one wot killed her. She was beggin' for it.'

'You're wasted in the force, Jo. You should have been an actress.' He narrowed his eyes. 'I can just see him now.'

'Then perhaps, Dr Levin,' she said, 'you'd do me the courtesy of telling me who it was.' She glanced back at the slab. 'Anything more?'

I only wish there was because he's a dangerous character, Jo,' Matthew warned. 'Turned on by sex and violence. Be careful.'

'I've always got Mike near by.'

'Make sure you have.'

He dried his hands on a paper towel. 'Now, how about lunch?'

She shook her head. 'Absolutely not. Report to Colclough then a visit to forty-five Jubilee Road.' She held out her hand. 'Bye.'

It was the turn of the two older children to be miserable. Ryan, the baby, was happy now that Christine had found a suitable milk and cereal mix, and Christine's seven-year-old daughter Sheila made a fine little mother. But Sharon's two other children, October and William, were unconvinced and kept up their demands to know where their real mother was.

'Where is she, Chris?' This time it was October who was asking, her blue eyes wide and still innocent.

Christine stared at her impatiently. 'I don't bloody know,' she said, the first prickings of uneasiness starting to make her irritable.

Sharon was a good mum. All right – the first night she might have been excited . . . having a good time. Maybe she'd had too much to drink and was too pissed to drive home. But two nights had gone by now, and she hadn't rung. For the thirtieth time Christine crossed the room to the telephone. Perhaps it was out of order. But the familiar burr of the dialling tone was loud. There was nothing wrong with her phone.

William Priest had started whimpering. 'Mummy . . . Mummy,' he kept saying. October's eyes began to fill with tears and the pair of them wailed in unison.

Chapter Four

Joanna called to see Chief Superintendent Arthur Colclough as soon as she arrived back at the station. He
was looking grim. The Super was a large man, over-
weight with big jowls and drooping cheeks that always
reminded her of a Staffordshire bulldog. Years of eating
the wrong food and sitting behind a desk had made his
body cumbersome and sluggish. But his mind was clear
and quick and Joanna was acutely aware that it was
largely to the Super that she owed her position. She
respected him. She also liked him.

'Sit down, Piercy, and fill me in,' he said.

'The body of a young woman,' she told him, 'no
more than thirty. A farmer found her lying on the
moors, not far off the Buxton road, dressed for a night
out.'

He nodded. 'How long had she been there?'

'A couple of days, the pathologist said, and that
matches up with the snow picture. It started on
Tuesday night. Driving was difficult on the moors after
about ten, according to the Met office . . .'

'Cause of death?'

'Strangulation.'

'When are we looking at?'

'Some time late on Tuesday night,' she said, and felt she needed to defend Matthew. 'It was difficult for Dr Levin to be absolutely sure, because of the sub-zero conditions. But the farmer was positive she wasn't there early on Tuesday evening.' She stopped. 'Besides, cars couldn't get through from about midnight until the plough cleared the road early the next morning. The picture I have is of a date some time Tuesday evening. She was picked up, assaulted, murdered and her body dumped.'

His eyes looked shrewd. 'And what were the findings of the PM?'

'She'd been garrotted,' she said slowly. 'A wire ligature that almost cut the neck, twisted with a length of sawn-off broomstick.'

Arthur Colclough frowned. 'Nasty,' he said. The one word spoke reams.

He looked at her. 'You've samples?'

'Raped first,' she said quietly.

'So it was sexual?'

'It looks like it.'

Colclough shifted his bulk in the chair. 'Have you got any suspects, Piercy?'

She shook her head. 'Not yet. I'll go round to her address this afternoon and set the wheels in motion.'

'Fine. And make use of the PNC2. I want to know if it links up with any other killings or rapes, both in this area and around the country.' He stopped. 'If it isn't a purely domestic business we'd better be very careful – don't you think?'

'Yes, sir.'

He peered at her. 'What's your gut feeling, Piercy?'

'I don't know, sir. I can only say . . .'

'Yes?' he prompted.

'I'm a bit uneasy,' she finished. 'Nothing in particular. It's just it was a very professional killing.' She met his eyes. 'I think your idea might bear fruit, sir, though' – she frowned – 'I don't recall anything like it.'

He nodded.

'There's something else, sir. The fact that the girl was dressed up to go out. A red dress – cheap but smart – a lot of make-up, high-heeled shoes. I just wonder if she was set up, invited out.'

'To be raped and then murdered?' Colclough looked appalled.

'It looks like it.' And the mention of the shoes reminded her. 'One of the shoes is missing. Korpanski is scouring the moors. But if we don't find it there's a possibility it's been kept as a souvenir.'

'Make that a priority, Piercy,' he said. 'Get the lads to scour that moor. If it's found up there – well, that's fine. But on the other hand . . .' His eyes were bright, 'It could lead you right to his door.'

And she agreed with him.

His attention moved back to her. 'You can have all the men you need, Piercy,' he said. 'All leave will be cancelled until you've got the killer.'

'Thank you, sir.'

'Sure you can handle it?'

'I'm happy – so far.'

Colclough was watching her. 'Do you have a name for this poor unfortunate?'

She nodded. 'Handbag found by the body. Credit cards, purse . . . Her name, we think, was Sharon

Priest. And we have an address – forty-five Jubilee Road. It's a large council estate on the edge of the moor.'

'So you'll start your investigations there?'

'Korpanski and I will go round this afternoon,' she said, 'look into her family, friends, boyfriends, husband, ex or current. I'll get the uniformed lads to ask around the bars and pubs, find out where she was going dressed so smartly.'

'Anything else?'

'No, but I think that's enough to start with,' she said. 'Then there are the shoe shops, clothes shops. Her dress looked fairly new. And there's her work – if she had a job.' She smiled at him. 'I've got plenty to be getting on with, sir. I'll probably link into the computer early this evening.'

Colclough jerked his head towards the window. 'What's going on on the moors?'

'The usual, sir,' she said. 'Fingertip search and stop the motorists.'

He stood up then, escorted her to the door. 'Fine. You're going to be busy.'

She smiled and watched his eyes twinkle.

'Good luck,' he said.

The children had at last become absorbed in a Walt Disney video. Christine Rattle watched them, smoke curling from her mouth as she pondered what the hell to do with them. She didn't have a key to Sharon's front door and she needed clean clothes for October and Ryan. William was no problem. She had given him something of Tarquine's to wear. She glanced across the road, wondering if she could get in through the back door, or if Sharon still kept a key under the flowerpot. The house was quiet, deserted, curtains drawn. And instinctively she knew it would not be Sharon who drew them back.

As she watched, a police car slid to a halt outside and almost in a daze Christine knew it meant bad news. She picked up the baby, stuck him on her hip, opened the front door and crossed the road.

Korpanski glowered at her. He hated sightseers. But Joanna stared. 'Hi, Chris,' she said.

Christine looked at her and felt a stab of fear. She jerked her head towards the silent house. 'What's goin' on?'

'Do you know her?'

Christine nodded at the baby on her hip. 'Been mindin' her kids,' she said. 'Now what's goin' on?'

'Got a key, love?'

Christine Rattle looked at the burly Detective Sergeant then she blinked. 'She used to keep one under the flowerpot,' she said. 'What is goin' on?'

Joanna made her decision quickly. 'You get inside, Mike,' she said. 'I'll talk to Christine.'

Together they walked back, across the road, towards Christine's house.

The children were still absorbed in the cartoon characters. Christine plonked the baby between them and told them to 'Mind 'im.' Then she shut the connecting door firmly and sat down opposite Joanna in the kitchen.

'Are you goin' to tell me, then?'

Christine was a thin woman with a hard face, premature lines, work-roughened bony hands and fuzzy, permed hair that lacked colour. But Joanna knew her well. She knew she was honest and punctilious and did a full day's work that would put many men to shame. Somehow on her meagre wages she afforded decency, clothes for her children, heating and food. And the house, Joanna had noticed, was spotless.

As was her own cottage ever since Christine had been coming round.

'Did you know Sharon well?' she began.

But Christine was too quick for her. 'What's *happened*?' she insisted.

Joanna swallowed. 'We're not sure,' she began.

Christine looked fierce. 'I was one of her best friends,' she said. 'I was mindin' her kids for her. If anything's happened I've got a right to be told.'

'We've found the body of a woman.'

Christine's face grew blank and she glanced around the kitchen. 'What about the kids?'

Joanna reached out and touched her hand. 'We aren't sure yet that it is Sharon.'

Christine looked at her dumbly.

'A woman's handbag was found on the moors,' Joanna continued. 'The contents suggest that it was Sharon Priest's.' She paused for a moment. 'Near the handbag was the body.'

'Oh my God.' Christine turned white. 'What did she look like?'

'Slim, dyed auburn hair – thick, styled, backcombed. She was wearing a dark red dress . . .'

She didn't need to say any more. Christine fumbled across the table for her bag, drew out a cigarette and lit it with shaking hands.

Joanna stood up and filled the kettle. 'I'll make you a cup of tea, Chris,' she said kindly.

Christine Rattle was fighting back tears. She sniffed and then looked at Joanna. 'What happened to her? Was it the snow?'

Joanna shook her head.

Christine stared at her. 'When?' she whispered.

'We think it was late on Tuesday night.'

Christine took a shaky drag from her cigarette. 'She was on a date,' she said. 'She was going out with someone.'

'Who?'

'I don't know his name,' she said, frowning. 'It was a guy she met through the personal column.'

'Had she been out with him before?'

Christine bit her lip. 'No,' she said. 'She hadn't met him. He'd been writing her letters. It was her first date. That's why I did her hair for her.' She dabbed her eyes with a tissue. 'And she wore her best dress. He told her to wear it.'

Joanna leaned forward. 'He rang her?'

Christine shook her head violently. 'He wrote. They both did – used the box number.'

'Which paper?'

'The *Evening Standard*.'

The door opened and was quickly closed again, and Christine stared at Joanna. 'What about the kids?' she asked. 'I can't manage them. What'll happen to them?'

'Please . . .' Joanna said, handing her a mug of strong, sweet tea. 'Don't worry. The Social Services can take over. Then usually relatives . . .'

Christine Rattle took a large sip of scalding tea. 'Not her mum,' she said. 'She could never cope with Sharon's three, especially Ryan. He's just a baby. Maybe the other two, but Ryan – no way.' She frowned. 'Tell me. What happened?'

'I can't give you all the details,' Joanna began, 'but the woman we found was murdered.'

Christine was staring at her through a wisp of blue cigarette smoke. 'She was so excited,' she said.

Joanna's mobile phone crackled. She answered it.

'Car found. Green Fiesta,' came the message. 'Check registration. X – X-ray; W – Whisky; O – Oscar. 4–3–6 – W – Whisky. Repeat . . . car park of the Quiet Woman . . .'

'Don't touch it,' she said, and, to Christine, 'Was Sharon in her car on Tuesday night?'

Christine nodded.

'Registration?' And Joanna read out the number-plate she had written down during the phone call.

Christine looked uncertain. 'I can't remember the number.' Joanna relayed the details down the phone. 'Check with Swansea.'

'Already have. Registered owner Sharon Priest . . . forty-five Jubilee Road . . .'

'Don't touch the inside. Get it to forensics. And I'll see you all later.'

She turned her attention back to Christine. 'Who was he?'

'It was just a date,' Christine said, pulling away at

61

her cigarette as though it was her lifeline. 'I told you. She hadn't been out with him before. She was lonely. She'd been on her own with the children. She wanted some excitement.'

She looked across the table at Joanna. 'Why shouldn't she have had some fun? She deserved it.'

'No reason,' Joanna soothed. 'No reason at all, except I don't call being killed fun, do you? And I know she didn't deserve what happened to her.'

Christine mopped her eyes again. 'Did she suffer?'

'No,' she said. She felt a lie was justified.

'Christine swallowed, tears flowing freely again. She sniffed and looked at Joanna. 'I can't believe it,' she said. 'The scum. The dirty, rotten scum. I suppose he came over a bit strong and she resisted?'

And again, although Joanna knew it had not been like that, she nodded.

'Now tell me everything you know about the man she had a date with.'

But Christine Rattle looked blank. 'I didn't know anything about him,' she said.

'Did you see a photograph?'

She shook her head.

'Well, where did he live?'

Christine looked panic-struck. 'I don't even know that. In his letters he just said it wasn't far.'

'But wasn't there an address?'

Blindly Christine shook her head again. They wrote to box numbers, like I said?

Joanna felt frustrated. 'You don't know *anything* about him?' she said incredulously.

Christine shook her head for a third time.

'Well, where had she arranged to meet him?'

Something like a dark, angry cloud crossed Christine's face. 'There's not many decent blokes here in Leek,' she said. 'Sharon had had a couple of boyfriends. One was married. One was just no good. And her ex was violent. He's been inside for ABH. So she put an advert in the paper, saying she wanted a good time. She had loads of replies.' Christine sounded almost envious. 'More than forty. Some of them sounded really nice. You know – decent and kind. And they didn't mind about the kids at all. Some of them.' She made an expression of extreme distaste. 'But some of them – you could tell what they was after. One, he made a great thing about her wearing high-heeled shoes and glamour-girl stuff.'

'Did he now?'

Christine nodded.

'Why did she pick out the one she met on Tuesday night?'

'She said . . .' Christine gazed at the tip of ash glowing on the end of her cigarette. 'She thought he sounded exciting.'

'What do you mean, exciting?'

'She said there was something about him – something mysterious. He said things.'

'What sort of things?'

'I don't know.' Christine looked embarrassed. 'Things about how he fancied her a lot. She didn't show me the letters. She kept herself to herself. Anyway, she thought she'd go out with him first. After all,' she said, dragging on another cigarette, 'what's the point of wasting your time with some old bugger if all the time Prince Charming's waiting for you in the glass coach?'

'Quite,' Joanna said drily. 'So what was the arrangement?'

'They was meeting at the Quiet Woman. He told her to get there for eight and then they'd go on for a meal.'

Joanna's mind returned to the stomach contents spilled out at the post mortem. She hadn't had that meal.

'You last saw her when?'

'About eight. She dropped the kids off at seven. I did her hair. She left at eight.'

'Did she come back at all during the evening?'

Christine slowly shook her head. 'No. She didn't. I know because I kept a watch on her house.' She flushed. 'I wasn't being nosey, but I was itching to know who he was.'

'So they were to meet at the Quiet Woman at eight?'

Christine nodded. 'He said he'd come in for her.' She looked as though suddenly struck by the thought. 'Was it definitely him?'

'We don't know,' Joanna said, 'but her car has been found at the Quiet Woman.' She stood up. 'Please, Christine,' she said. 'Think. Was there anything else about this man? Anything at all?'

Christine blinked and stared ahead of her for a long time before speaking. 'There *was* something funny,' she said slowly. 'There *was*. Me and Sharon,' she licked her lips, 'we got the feeling he already knew her.'

'How?'

'He said . . . oh – I can't remember the exact words.

In one he said something about, about her dark hair –
and looking stunning in red.'

'You're sure?'

'Something like that.' Christine stubbed out her
cigarette. 'But the weirdest thing was that he knew
her name. When he wrote to her he said "Dear Sharon."
And he said she wouldn't have to drive that battered
old Fiesta for much longer.' She watched Joanna carefully. 'We thought it was funny at the time.' She blinked
back tears. 'She said it made her feel a bit creepy –
watched. You know. But she was still excited, though.
She still wanted to meet him.'

'Yes,' Joanna said. 'I do know.' She sighed. 'We'll
need to sort something out for her children. How many
are there?'

'Three. October, she's four, then there's William,
two. And lastly there's a baby, Ryan. He's only six
months old.' Christine looked even more upset. 'I don't
suppose they'll remember their mummy, will they?'

How could she expect Joanna to have an answer
to this? 'I don't know.'

'Christine . . .' Joanna said tentatively, knowing she
had to ask one of the most difficult questions of a
friend. She had underestimated her.

With a resigned air Christine stood up. 'I know
what you're going to ask me,' she said. 'To identify her.'
She stopped and sniffed. 'It'll give me nightmares but
I'll do it,' she said. 'I'll do it for her because I was her
friend. And I'll do it for them kids in there. And
because the sooner you're sure it was her the sooner
you'll nail the bastard what did it. I'll identify her,

provided she isn't all cut about.' She looked at Joanna.
'She isn't – is she?'

'No. No – she's quite neat and tidy. And it won't
take long. Don't worry.'

There were other points she had to clear up. 'Who
was her next of kin?'

'I don't know.' Christine looked confused. 'She was
married once, to a guy named Sam. Sam Finnigan. She
left him because he beat her about.' For some reason
she refused to meet Joanna's eyes. 'He's the father of
two of her children – but not Ryan. She had Ryan just
before Paul Agnew – that's the boyfriend she lived with
after Finnigan – after he kicked her out.'

'So is Paul Agnew Ryan's father?'

Christine shook her head. 'No, at least not that I
could ever work out. She never really told me, but
I think Ryan's dad was married. That's why Agnew
gave her the boot. She was havin' an affair.'

'Who with?'

Christine made a face. 'Close as the grave she was
about that one. She never told no one.'

And that, it seemed, was that.

'Where will I find Paul Agnew?' Joanna asked.

'He's got an oatcake shop in the High Street. But
he lives in a flat in the town somewhere. I don't know
where.'

'Where does Finnigan live?'

'I don't know where he lives now. Rents rooms
somewhere, Sharon said. She told me that was why he
didn't see much of the kids. Nowhere for them to play.'
Christine made a face. 'Just an excuse, if you ask me.'

'And her parents?'

'Just a mum, I think. I never heard her talk about her dad. But Sharon and her mum don't have a lot to do with each other. Not since Ryan was born. Funnily enough her mum quite liked Sam Finnigan. She was mad with Sharon for the business with the married man.' She thought for a minute. 'I think she was a nursing auxiliary somewhere or other. I'm not sure where.'

On the way out they passed through the sitting room. Christine indicated a small girl in grubby blue dungarees holding the hand of a little boy in a red jersey and jeans.

'These is Sharon's,' she said. 'October and William. And that,' she indicated a baby crawling towards the television set, 'that's Ryan.'

Joanna looked curiously at Ryan. There was something different about the child. He was plumper, pinker, rounder – a handsome baby with bright eyes that despite his youth looked out to the world with a knowing intelligence which seemed lacking from either his sister or brother. Correction – his half-sister and half-brother.

Still puzzling, she left Christine's house and crossed the road to number forty-five.

Mike had let himself in through the back door with the key he had found underneath the flowerpot. He'd drawn back the curtains and was standing in the middle of the cold room. He looked at her as she walked in.

'I don't know what I'm looking for,' he complained.

The house smelt stale. Unlike Christine, Sharon had not been a scrupulous housekeeper. There was an unpleasant smell of cooking fat mingled with cigarette smoke, old perfume and hair lacquer. Toys were strewn around the room.

On the coffee table, in the centre, was a collection of make-up, mascara, foundation cream, a palette of eye colour and a mirror in a pink, plastic frame.

'Was she killed here?' Joanna asked.

'I don't think so.'

'Any sign of a man?'

Mike shook his head. 'Plenty of signs of kids,' he said, 'in the kitchen. All over the place. Nappies, toys, kids' clothes. I haven't been upstairs yet.'

Joanna wandered through to the kitchen. It was untidy – a sinkful of washing up, an opened can of baked beans, a half-eaten loaf of white bread, its wrapper torn apart.

They walked upstairs and found the children's bedroom, strewn with toys, bunks with gaudy, bright quilt covers. And in the other bedroom was a double bed and a cot. So Ryan slept in his mother's room. And on his cot was an expensive satin and lace duvet. Not the cheap bedding of the other two. Joanna stared at the cot and again she was puzzled.

She crossed the room and opened the wardrobe. It was full of clothes, all for a slightly built woman.

Back in the sitting room Mike was looking at a newspaper marked with red pen.

'Jo, look at this.'

It was the local evening paper, an edition almost

three weeks old. Ringed in red felt-tipped pen was the shape of a love heart.

Woman In Red looking for romance and sparkle.
Wants a really good time with Prince Charming.
Please apply BOX 397.

Joanna read it three times before speaking, then she met Mike's eyes. 'This looks like it, then,' she said. 'According to Christine, she had a date with Prince Charming last night.'

Mike put the paper down. 'It was in here,' he said.

The shoe box had once held a pair of high-heeled black shoes – size 5 – according to the panel on the side. Now it contained a bundle of letters – most of them addressed in florid handwriting to Box 397. All of them had been opened.

'Bring the box with you, Mike,' she said, 'and get the SOCOs to comb through the house. Then ring the station and get the Social Services round to Christine Rattle's. We'd better go straight to the Quiet Woman. It seems they've found Sharon Priest's car.'

Chapter Five

The Quiet Woman was living up to its name that afternoon. It was a small pub on the edge of the town with bowed windows which looked out on to the street. They found its car park at the back.

The car was neatly parked and gift wrapped with police ribbon.

Sergeant Barraclough walked towards her. 'Inspector,' he said. 'We haven't touched it except to try the handles.'

'They were locked?'

He nodded. 'It looks to me like she parked it here, locked it and went for a drink.'

She nodded at him. 'But with whom?' she asked. 'That's the question.'

Barraclough glanced back at the battered Fiesta. 'The guy that killed her,' he said. 'Went for a nice drinky, followed by sex in the car. Then murder.'

She peered through the windows. 'Not in this car.'

'Makes most dates seem kind of tame, doesn't it?'

There was no answer to that.

Joanna glanced back at the pub. 'Have you spoken to them?'

'Not much,' Barraclough said. 'Just mentioned it

had connections with a major incident. I thought I'd leave it to you.'

'Thanks.' Joanna looked curiously at the car, peered in through the window. On the passenger side lay a thick, pink anorak, neatly folded. It looked designed to keep snow out.

Mike frowned at it. 'On such a cold night,' he said, 'why leave the coat in the car? Her dress was a skimpy thing. Bare shoulders. It wouldn't have kept her warm. She'd have got cold even walking from the car to the pub.'

'It's easy to see you don't understand women!' she said, looking pityingly at Mike. 'Pink anorak over your best red dress?'

He frowned at her.

'The two colours clash.'

He laughed. 'Mind you, Joanna,' he said, 'if it was the chap from the ad that might have been the way he knew it was her. The red dress.'

She nodded. 'It's possible. But from what Christine Rattle told me, he'd have no trouble recognizing her because he already knew her. Mike,' she said, 'when we get back to the station I want you to stick a pair of gloves on and study his letters. If there's anything there that gives us the slightest hint who our Prince Charming is I want to know about it.'

She spoke to Barraclough then. 'OK.' She nodded. 'Get the car on a low-loader and down to the police pound and we'll let the forensics boys have a look at it.'

But as she walked around to the front of the pub she said to Mike, 'I don't think we'll get much from it, if anything. I'm convinced she locked the car and went into the pub. And that was the last contact she had with the vehicle.'

The black painted front door was firmly closed. Mike picked up the knocker and dropped it loudly. They stood back and waited.

A girl opened it just a fraction. 'What do you want?'

'Police,' Mike said, holding up his ID card. 'We want to ask some questions in connection with a major incident.'

The girl's eyes opened wide. 'What major incident?'

'Can we come in, love?'

The girl nodded and stood back.

The pub was dark inside and pungent with the stink of stale tobacco and spilt beer. They were obviously still cleaning up. Glasses lined the bar and the girl was holding a red and white check teatowel.

'Any chance I could speak to the landlady?'

'She ain't here. What's it about?'

'The car that was found in your car park.' Joanna felt this was a decent starting point.

The girl blinked. 'What's the problem?' She gave them a world-weary glance. 'Another one stolen?'

Joanna shook her head and the girl picked up a glass from the sink and began polishing it. 'What, then?'

She sounded almost bored by the whole business.

'The woman who drove it here.'

'Look.' The girl frowned. I don't know who drove it here. I don't see people parking their cars. They put them round the back or across the road. Jack the bloody Ripper could have drove it 'ere for all I know.'

'It was a young woman who drove it here,' Joanna

said steadily, 'on Tuesday night.' She looked at the barmaid. 'Perhaps you weren't on duty that night?'

The girl nodded. 'I was here. What did she look like?'

'Slim, in a dark red dress. Auburn shoulder-length hair.' She stopped. 'I think you might remember her. It was snowing but she wasn't wearing a coat. Her shoulders were bare.'

The girl's curiosity was finally aroused. 'I do remember her. She was sitting over there.' She indicated the plush seat nearest the door. 'She was here for ages, waiting for her boyfriend. She kept staring out of the window.' She paused. 'I reckoned it must be someone she'd fancied a long time.'

'Why?' Mike's question was brusque and the barmaid looked annoyed.

'Because she went to the toilets twice to do her hair and put more lipstick on.' She giggled. 'And she looked nervous. Her hand was shaking holding her glass.'

She stopped suddenly, as though her memory had been pricked. She moved her gaze from Joanna to Mike.

'What's happened to her?' she asked.

'Did the bloke come in the end?' It was Mike, still sounding impatient.

'Sort of,' the barmaid said reluctantly. 'At least I suppose it was the bloke she'd been waiting for.' She stared out of the window. 'Pulls up outside – noisy as hell – flashes his lights straight into the lounge. She stands up, walks to the door. Bloke standing there. She says something to him, and off they go.'

'What did he look like?'

'I dunno.' The barmaid shrugged her shoulders. 'He was wearing an anorak, hood up. I didn't think there was anything funny about it,' she said defensively. 'It was a bloody freezing night. I couldn't see his face. I was busy. And I didn't really look. He was slim.' She glanced at Mike. 'Slimmer than you. Quite tall.' Again she looked at Mike. 'Your sort of height. She went off with him. That's all I know.' She looked helplessly at Joanna. 'Well, I didn't know, did I? I didn't know something was going on.' She screwed her eyes up. 'Anyway,' she said, 'what *was* goin' on?'

When neither of them replied she said more aggressively, 'Come on, I'll read it all in the evenin' paper.'

'The girl's been found dead,' Joanna said reluctantly. 'The body on the moors. It was her.'

The barmaid looked disbelievingly from one to the other. 'I don't believe it,' she said. 'She just looked ordinary . . . normal.'

'She didn't know she was about to be killed,' Mike said sarcastically. 'She thought she was on a date.'

The girl blinked. 'I don't think there was anything I could have done.'

'It's all right.' Joanna was getting too familiar with this defensive attitude to crime. 'Of course you didn't know. But just think carefully. Was there anything – anything at all – that might help us identify this man? Had you ever seen him before?'

The girl stopped, then shook her head slowly. 'He wasn't one of our regulars. At least I don't think he was.' Her face filled with uncomfortable fascination. 'What exactly happened to her?'

'We can't release details,' Joanna said.

'I never knew anyone who got murdered,' she said in awe. 'A suicide, and a friend of my brother's who got paralyzed in a car accident. But murder . . .'

Mike glanced at Joanna and she knew what he was thinking. What a ghoul.

She looked at the girl. 'Do you think you might be able to get together with the other people serving behind the bar that night and draw a plan of who was here – where they sat, what time they arrived, what time they left?'

The barmaid's eyes were round. 'I think so.' She nodded. 'Between us we might manage.'

'Good.' Joanna felt pleased. So far so good. Then she turned to the barmaid again. 'And don't forget to fill in even people who dropped in for one drink earlier and then left. They might have seen her sitting alone and come back later for her.'

She stopped. 'How many people were serving behind the bar that night?'

'Two of us girls,' the barmaid said, 'and Pablo. He owns the place. He's Spanish.' The girl swallowed. 'Can I ask,' she said timidly, 'what time was she killed?'

'Some time during the evening,' Joanna said, 'before the snow came down.'

'Can I ask something else?'

The barmaid was beginning to look frightened. 'Do you think it might have been someone who drinks here regularly?'

Joanna met her eyes. 'We don't know,' she said. 'We just don't know.'

*

'Mike,' she said when they were outside, 'we'll have to get the boys to take statements from everyone drinking at the Quiet Woman on Tuesday night plus the three staff.' She paused. 'I know at the moment we're assuming the man she left the pub with – the man she had a date with – was the killer. But it's a dangerous assumption. It's not necessarily true. She could have had a perfectly legitimate date, then been killed by someone else that night.'

Mike's eyes narrowed. 'But her car was still there,' he said.

'I know that,' she said, irritated. 'I'm just saying. We must take this investigation one small step at a time.'

Mike grunted.

'So let's start the ball rolling. Set up an incident room and let's get those statements ready to read through. If we can get a decent description of the man from someone at the Quiet Woman that night we have a head start. Maybe someone was outside the pub at the time when his car pulled up. Or it's possible someone was entering the pub at the same time he did.'

'It was a very cold night,' Mike reminded her. 'I don't suppose people were hanging around.'

'No, but there's always a chance,' Joanna said. 'We've had some nice surprises before. And some lucky breaks. So it's back to leg work and statements, Mike.'

'Great,' he said. 'My favourite hobby – getting statements from folk who keep their ears and eyes shut when there's a crime around.'

Joanna laughed. 'Stop grumbling.'

'Still.' He brightened up. 'We've got DNA from the semen.'

She drummed her fingers on the steering wheel. 'Are you suggesting we take semen samples from every bloke around Leek?' She met his eyes. 'We don't have the powers to do that. We have to find a suspect. Then we can move. Don't be impatient,' she warned.

She started the engine and let out the clutch.

He was silent for the first half of the journey, then suddenly he said, 'If I'm going to be helping the boys collect statements all afternoon what are you going to be up to?'

'The morgue,' she said grimly. 'I promised Christine I'd drive her down. Someone has to identify the body.'

He looked at her curiously. 'How do you know her so well? I wouldn't have thought she moved in the same circles as you and that solicitor chap.'

'God, Mike,' she spluttered. 'Don't be such a snob. She's a very nice person.'

He ignored the comment.

'She cleans the cottage for me,' she said. 'And a bloody good job she makes of it too. She's also my friend.'

Mike nodded, and the action infuriated her even more.

'Then I'll have to talk to the Coroner,' she continued, 'and I thought I'd better see what the forensic psychologist has to offer.'

'You still believe in all that psychology mumbo-jumbo?'

'Yes, I do.'

Mike shrugged his shoulders. 'You're entitled to your own opinions, I suppose.'

'Yes – I am.' She smiled. 'However, I shall still rely on pure science and traditional police methods. I'll finish the day with my old friend H.O.L.M.E.S.'

He grinned. 'Lucky you,' he said. 'Never was much into computers myself. Anyway, this is a local crime, surely. Someone who dated a local girl and killed her.'

She took her eyes off the road to look at Mike's square face. 'You saw the cable twisted round the broom handle. The way that girl was killed. Do you really think that expert job was the work of an amateur?'

'Don't you?' He stared at her, appalled.

Slowly she shook her head. 'No,' she said. 'I don't. I have the most awful feeling he's done it before. Maybe just the rape with a touch of bondage. But I'm worried, and tonight I'm going to plug into the computer and look at other stranglings . . . garrottings . . . rapes . . . complaints of violence associated with sex.'

'Oh, shit.' Mike settled back in his seat, gnawing the tip of his thumb.

They drove back to the station in silence.

There was an envelope lying on her desk when she arrived at her office. It was addressed to her, written in neat capitals. Without any sort of premonition she slit the top with a knife and pulled out the note.

She read it twice before crumpling it up and dropping it into the bin.

It was now three forty-five. She had arranged to pick Christine up at four.

'Who left the note?' she asked the Duty Sergeant on her way out.

But Jane had been cunning. No one had seen anything. The note had been found on the floor with Joanna's name on it.

Christine was silent for most of the journey to the mortuary and Joanna left her to her thoughts. She had dressed up for the occasion in a flowered pink suit and was shivering. Joanna leaned forward and switched the car heater full on.

It was only as they neared the hospital that Christine started to speak. 'Joanna,' she said quietly, 'I'm a bit worried about this. I've never seen a dead person before.' She swallowed. 'Does she look much different?' She was pale, twisting her fingers around her wrists.

Joanna felt a rush of sympathy for her. 'I never saw her alive,' she said softly. But she looks OK. No blood. It won't take long. We just want you to take a quick glance at her face. We need to be absolutely sure it's her.'

Christine moved her hand in a quick, helpless gesture.

'She didn't look a mess, did she – when you found her?' She stopped. 'She cared, you know, how she looked.' Her lip trembled slightly. 'I suppose some people might say she was a bit vain. Spent ages on her hair, I did, that night.' She looked at Joanna. 'She was so sure he was going to be something really fantastic. George Michael, the Chippendales – all rolled into one. I did warn her. Sharon, I said. Don't expect too much.'

She gave a dry laugh. 'But that's what she got, wasn't it? Too much.'

Joanna said nothing. Such a vivid picture was emerging of this young woman she had only ever seen dead.

As the car drew up outside the mortuary Joanna spoke again. 'Christine, we're going to want to know all the details of Sharon's life – even some you might have considered private or confidential – so that we can trace everyone who had a connection with her.'

Christine nodded. 'Yeah, all right,' she said. 'I thought you'd want to know. But it was him, wasn't it? The guy from the advert.'

'Yes,' Joanna said cautiously. 'We think it probably was, but you thought he might already know her. It isn't impossible someone answered the advert knowing it was Sharon who had put it in.'

Christine dropped her head into her hands. 'I can hardly bear to think,' she said, then looked up. 'Have you spoken to her mum yet?'

'Only very briefly on the telephone. She wasn't keen on the identification. I didn't get very far,' she said. 'You said they weren't close.'

Christine shook her head.

'Can I ask you something?' Joanna was pulling the car into the hospital entrance. 'Sharon Priest was married to Sam Finnigan. But she and the children share the surname Priest.' She looked at Christine Rattle. 'Why?'

'She wouldn't change her name,' Christine said. 'Hated the name Finnigan. So she kept the name Priest and all her kids are called Priest too.'

'Thanks.' It had set Joanna's mind at rest.

Christine stared down at the white face of her friend. Then she did a strangely moving thing. Bending over and kissing the pale cheek, she spoke to the still figure.

'Don't you worry, Sharon,' she said softly. 'I'll do everything I can to help them get him. And I promise you. We will get him. I know we will.'

Joanna felt suddenly awkward. She wished she too could have made that promise to the dead girl. But years in the police force had taught her. Promises of 'nailing' people, just deserts, suitable prison sentences. These were pledges she was unable to make and keep. The only thing she could say with truth was that she would try – long and hard.

Christine pulled the sheet back up over her friend's face. 'Sleep now, Sharon,' she said and turned away.

Then she straightened up and looked at Joanna. 'I'm glad I came,' she said.

There was a small interview room halfway along the corridor. Containing a few seats, a coffee machine and a porthole in the door, it was a private room, where she had occasionally snatched moments with Matthew. Now she led Christine Rattle to it, inserted money into the coffee machine and handed her a polystyrene cup.

'I wanted to talk informally,' she said, 'away from the station and not at your house. Tell me about

81

Sharon. Tell me about her life. What sort of person was she?'

As Christine spoke, her thin face changed and became fierce. 'She was an ordinary person,' she said. 'Kind . . . really loyal. And she was a good mum.' She looked at Joanna with a kind of pity. 'You wouldn't know,' she said, 'not having kids. But it's really difficult trying to bring them up decent when you're on your own.'

'But the children had a father.'

'Sam Finnigan,' Christine said scornfully. 'A lot of bloody use he was. Fine at losing his temper and swiping them when they got in the way of the telly.'

'I see. And what about Agnew?'

Christine looked uneasy.

'Off the record,' Joanna said deliberately.

It seemed to convince Christine. 'He's high as a kite half the time. See . . .' she paused, 'the trouble was for Sharon she never met anyone decent – normal.' She looked even more angry and fumbled in her bag until she found her cigarettes. 'The one reasonable guy she met was married. Mind you . . .' She lit the cigarette and took a deep puff, blowing the smoke out with a whistle and picking a piece of stray tobacco from her tongue. 'He was good to her, although . . . well . . .' She looked up, caught sight of a face in the porthole. 'Who the hell's he?'

Matthew was grinning at them through the glass.

Joanna stood up hastily. 'Excuse me,' she said and walked outside.

Matthew spoke first. 'I wondered if you'd be

bringing someone in to identify the girl,' he said. 'Why didn't you ring and tell me you were coming?'

'It's all right. The mortuary attendant looked after us.'

'I'd have looked after you. Joanna,' he said. 'Please – can we talk some time?'

She touched his arm. 'There isn't any point, Matthew. We've been through this. You made your choice. I just hope you're happy.'

He raised his eyebrows. 'Do you?'

She flushed.

'Joanna. Look . . .' He brushed a stray hair from her cheek. 'I want you.'

He was so close she could feel his body warmth, his breath on her cheek, the nearness of him . . .

'I had a letter from Jane this afternoon,' she said.

He looked startled. 'What?'

'Unsigned.'

He stared at her.

'The usual insults, I can leave you to guess what they were. I don't enjoy this, Matthew.'

'Joanna, I'm so sorry.'

She turned to go back into the room. 'Just ask her to leave me alone,' she said.

His hand was on her shoulder. 'Meet me,' he said, but she shook her head.

'No.'

'I'll come to the cottage one night.'

'It's better you don't.' She sighed. 'I'm sorry, Matthew. It's really not going to work.'

'You don't understand.' His voice was hard and urgent. 'We came to a truce – for Eloïse . . .'

Now she turned and her voice was equally hard. 'Then bloody well stick to it.'

She returned to the room, conscious that he was staring after her.

'What a dish,' said Christine when the door was closed. 'Is he your boyfriend?'

'No,' Joanna said. 'Just an old friend. He works here.'

Christine gave her a world-wise look. 'I see,' she said. 'But he is a bit of all right.'

Joanna laughed.

'What a shame,' Christine said sagely. 'They're all married – all the nice ones. They get nabbed. And then the wives, they hold on.'

'Yes,' Joanna echoed. 'They hold on.'

Christine lit another cigarette and spoke with it dangling precariously from her lips. 'Like the guy Sharon was seeing. His wife . . . she wasn't going to let him go.' She paused to take a few puffs at the cigarette. 'No way.'

Joanna risked a swift glance up at the porthole. Matthew had gone.

Christine carried on talking. 'You see, all she wanted was a little bit of sparkle in her life, you know. She looked after her kids. All she wanted was someone to care for her a bit.' She ground her cigarette into the ashtray. 'It isn't fair. It's all wrong.'

She stared at Joanna. 'And now this.'

'Then help us, Christine. Tell me about her ex-husband,' Joanna said. 'He was the father of her two oldest, you said.'

'October and William. They split up after he came

home from night work and found her with this bloke.'
She giggled and for a moment looked young and mischievous. 'They wasn't even up to anything. They was
asleep. Anyway, Sam lost his rag then. Broke her jaw.
She got him for it – ABH and he was warned to keep
away from her. But when he got drunk he'd come
round and make a nuisance of himself all over again,
like he couldn't leave her alone.'

'He was violent towards her?'

Christine nodded. 'Verbals and physicals,' she said.

'Did he ever attempt rape?'

The question seemed to confuse Christine. She
thought for a minute then shook her head, her eyes
flickering towards the door. Eventually she answered.
'Not as I know of,' she said. 'Violence, yes, but I don't
think . . . No – nothing sexual. Then she moved in with
Paul Agnew.' She seemed anxious to move away from
the subject of Finnigan.

Joanna interrupted her. 'Was Agnew the man Finnigan found her in bed with?'

'No.' Christine shook her head. 'I never did know
who that bloke was.' She sniffed. 'Sharon made a joke
about it. He ran out of the bedroom and right out of
her life. She says she never saw him again.'

'Did you believe that?'

The woman shook her head. 'Sharon could be
really secretive sometimes. All I know is she was on
her own for a while before she moved in with Agnew,
so the bloke couldn't have amounted to much, could
he?'

Joanna kept her private thoughts to herself and
instead returned to Agnew. 'And were they happy?'

85

'Were they hell.' Christine lit another cigarette. 'Not for a minute they weren't. I don't know why she bothered with him. For a start he was nearly always stoned. Although he isn't a bad bloke. He isn't violent like Sam, or anything weird. But I do know there was something peculiar.'

Joanna looked up.

'He's – well . . .' Surprisingly she flushed. 'Nothing to do with her being killed.' She paused. 'I don't think it was him.'

And for now Joanna was content to leave it at that.

'But she split up with him?'

'She was pregnant,' Christine said reluctantly. 'He threw her out.'

Joanna remembered what Christine had told her. 'You said before that Sharon was having an affair, but surely the baby *could* have been Agnew's?'

Christine shrugged her shoulders. 'Don't ask me,' she said. 'He threw her out. That's all I know.'

'Who was the man she was involved with? What's his name?'

She shook her head. 'I don't know,' she said. 'I really don't. All I know is he was married.' She looked at Joanna. 'I've told you. Sharon was quite close like that. She could really keep secrets. I've never known anyone – certainly not any of my girlfriends – who could keep a secret like her. She never told on him.'

'She must have said something – anything – that'll help us identify him. Christine,' Joanna said, 'you realize he is a suspect.'

'Well . . . She said they made love in his car.'

Christine giggled. 'She said it was really difficult, although it was a flash car.'

'Didn't she know the make?'

'Oh, she knew it all right, but she didn't tell me. Just flash. That's all she said.'

Joanna sighed. What if Sharon had kept the secret of her lover for long enough? Threatened to tell his wife? Might he then have decided to kill her?

'She split from him too,' Christine said. 'I don't know why. But it was something to do with Ryan, not long after he was born.' She frowned. 'Sharon was really bloody angry about it. Kept saying she felt used, taken advantage of. That was when she first thought about putting the ad in the paper. I think it was partly to spite him. You know – to prove she'd get someone else. I think Sharon really liked him.'

She sat quietly for a moment, contemplating. Then she looked at Joanna. 'Not much of a life, was it? She was always worried about money and the kids. I hardly ever saw her laughing. Her idea of fun was a fag, some chips and a good romantic film on the telly.' She dabbed again at her cheek and rolled the tissue up in a ball.

Joanna took Sam Finnigan's and Paul Agnew's addresses and relayed all the information back to the station. She dropped Christine back at her house, then turned her car towards the station and an evening in front of her computer screen. The PNC2 was a new link which gave access to major crimes country wide. It had only been in place for a couple of years but it had already proved useful in a number of cases where crime had crossed police boundaries. She sat and tapped in details . . .

It was more than two hours later that she pushed her chair back from the desk. She caught sight of her face in the mirror, pale and tired, black rings beneath both eyes.

She left her office and found Mike still working at his desk, studying some of Sharon's letters.

He looked up. 'What is it, Jo?'

'I think he's done it before,' she said. 'I'll have to ring the Super.'

Mike shook his head. 'Surely not,' he said. 'Not in this area, he hasn't. There's been nothing round here like this before. I'm sure. I'd remember,' he added.

She sat him down in front of the computer terminal and pressed a few keys to bring up witnesses statements from a previous crime. She had selected the cases quite carefully. Capital crimes against women involving rape. And she had kept within a fifty-mile radius.

Mike watched her press the keys, her slim fingers with short, shaped nails agile across the board, her hand occasionally passing over her mouth as she waited for the computer to catch up with her demands.

She leaned forward to stare at the screen and cupped her chin in her hand. At last she found the statements that had excited and at the same time depressed her, then she looked up at him without saying a word. He stared, not at her but at the screen.

'It was him all right,' was all he said.

And he picked up the telephone himself and dialled Arthur Colclough's home telephone number.

*

Superintendent Colclough had just finished a hearty dinner of steak and mushrooms. He would have liked chips but had settled for the new potatoes his wife put in front of him, compensating by smothering them with butter. He had ignored his wife's disapproving look and muttered comments about cholesterol. Chips tomorrow, he was thinking, when the phone rang.

'Detective Inspector Piercy, sir,' she said, before apologizing for disturbing him at home. 'I can't be absolutely sure . . . but . . .'

'What is it, Piercy?' he asked testily. 'I'm just having my tea.'

'Sharon Priest wasn't the first one,' she said quietly. 'I think he's done it before.'

'What?' The shock made his voice squeak.

'He's killed before, sir. I'm pretty sure.'

Chapter Six

It was exactly twenty-five minutes later when the door swung open and Colclough marched in, heavy on his feet.

'What's all this about, Piercy?' His eyebrows were meeting in the middle, a sure sign of his bad temper. He gave Mike a curt nod. 'Still here, Korpanski?'

Then his attention focused on Joanna and the grey screen on the desk. 'Well,' he said. 'And why haven't we been alerted if there's a serial killer romping around?'

'As far as I can tell, sir,' she said, 'he isn't exactly a serial killer. I've connected one unsolved rape and murder with him.' She pressed a few keys. 'Macclesfield,' she said, peering into the screen. 'Eighteen months ago . . . A young woman of twenty-eight, called Stacey Farmer.' She paused to look up at Colclough, who was leaning over behind her and frowning.

'Like Sharon, she had put an ad in the lonely hearts column of the local paper. Here . . .' She pressed a couple more keys. 'This is the ad. "Help – Frustrated, bored, single mum seeks adventure with Superman lookalike." And she gave a box number too.'

She continued. 'Stacey had more than twenty

replies. But the one that interested the local police was this one.' Again her fingers danced across the keys.

'*I'm more handsome than Superman, more sexy and much more adventurous. Meet me at 8 p.m. at the Hayrick, Tuesday night.*'

The letter was signed with a capital S.

Joanna looked at Colclough and then back at Mike. 'Stacey kept the date. According to the barmaid, she sat in the corner of the pub, alone, until half past eight.'

She looked at them. 'Remember, Sharon was kept waiting.'

Mike spoke up. 'Perhaps he'd been watching from outside.'

She shrugged. 'Maybe. Anyway, at half past eight a man walked in. According to statements from the barmaid and drinkers at the pub that night, he was of medium height, medium build and was wearing a dark anorak with the hood pulled up. It was a rainy night and no one thought anything of it. He crossed to Stacey, spoke briefly and they left together.' She paused. 'She was never seen alive again. Her body was found two days later, dumped on the edge of Macclesfield Forest. She'd been raped and then garrotted.'

Now Joanna had no need of the computer. These next facts she would never forget. 'A thin, twisted steel cable had been used, together with a short length of a wooden broom handle to lever the cable.'

She watched Colclough's face. 'Stacey was very like Sharon Priest. Sparkly, physically attractive, deeply frustrated by the restrictions of bringing up a young family alone, desperately wanting some excitement in her life.'

Colclough blinked 'She certainly got that, didn't she?'

Joanna nodded.

'Well, Piercy,' he said, 'you'd better get over to Macclesfield and talk to the investigating officers.'

She nodded again, then added, 'In this case there was no shortage of suspects, sir. A little like Sharon, Stacey had plenty of men in her life. Only none of them led anywhere. They started off with four or five prime suspects. But no one was ever charged with the murder. It remains on their files.'

Both men were watching her now and she could read their minds.

Colclough cleared his throat noisily and muttered something about not liking unsolved murders on his patch, then he said, 'Do you think he's a Leek man, Piercy?'

She stopped and took a deep breath. 'I don't know. But I am sure he already knew Sharon. I don't think – for him at least – that it was a blind date.'

Colclough raised his eyebrows. 'On what grounds?'

'According to Christine, when he replied to Sharon's advert he told her to wear her best dress. He told her he didn't live very far away, although they had always used box numbers.'

'The paper's distributed all around the Potteries,' Mike objected.

'True, but he knew the Quiet Woman. And he said she would look stunning in red.'

'She called herself the woman in red.'

'He mentioned her dark hair. Besides, there's Sharon's instinct. She had a feeling he knew her. He knew she drove a battered Fiesta. And, strongest of all, sir,' she said, 'he knew her name, even though she never used it in her letters.'

Colclough sat down heavily, breathing hard. His blue eyes looked tired, but bright. He looked like an aged but alert bulldog. 'Let's get this quite straight, Piercy,' he said slowly, 'so I'm absolutely clear. You believe that the man who answered Stacey Farmer's advert in the lonely hearts column was the man who killed her.'

'That isn't my assumption,' she said quickly. 'It was the conclusion of the officers investigating the case.' She quoted from the statements recorded on the computer. 'An unknown male assailant following an assignation made through the lonely hearts column in the local paper—'

'All right,' Colclough said hastily. 'And you believe the same man answered Sharon Priest's ad, and then killed her. But you think he already knew her.' He stared at her. 'Just be careful, Piercy,' he said. 'Be careful you aren't restricting your investigations too much . . . keeping the field too narrow.'

'I'll start with boyfriends of Sharon Priest's,' she said firmly. 'And if I get no convictions there, then will be the time to move on.'

Colclough nodded, then turned to Mike. 'What do you think about that?'

'Seems pretty sensible to me.'

Colclough thought for a moment, then, 'All right, both of you,' he said.

'We'll know more definitely tomorrow when we compare DNA samples from the two cases,' she said.

'In the meantime I don't feel we can afford to ignore any avenue – certainly nothing connected with Sharon Priest's private life.'

She grinned at Colclough. 'After all, just think how embarrassing it would be if we were hunting high and low for some mysterious serial killer and it turned out to be Sharon's ex-husband all the time.'

'I'm glad you can see the funny side, Piercy,' Arthur Colclough said testily. 'Sometimes I have my doubts about your sense of humour.' He heaved a great sigh. 'Was there anything else?'

'There is one thing that worries me,' she said slowly. 'It might be irrational. Lots of women advertise in the personal columns. Quite a few of these fit this pattern – lonely, single-parent mums.' She stopped. 'I haven't got any figures but a few have subsequently gone missing. I hope,' she said, 'that Stacey and Sharon aren't the tip of an iceberg. It just bugs me. What if others who were put down as missing persons actually fell victim to the same man and we just haven't unearthed their bodies?'

'Why go fretting about other missing women, Piercy?' Colclough scowled. 'You've got enough of a problem nabbing the guy who killed Sharon and then proving it was the same bugger who got Stacey.'

She knew he was right to steer her back to the original murder.

'So who have you got so far in your bag of suspects?'

'Well,' she said slowly. 'There was no shortage of men in Sharon's life, and some of them are choice customers.' She grinned at them. 'You can take your pick. There was a violent ex-husband who came home one night to find her in bed with a so far unidentified man, a co-habitee who I'm very curious about, a married lover who no one knows anything about. Incidentally, it's possible that he's the father of her youngest child.' She sighed. 'As I said, no shortage of men – just like Stacey Farmer.'

'But with all those men in her life she still put an advert in the paper for one.' Colclough looked puzzled. 'Why?'

'Because she didn't exactly have what my mum would call a good steady relationship with any of them,' Joanna said. 'The violent ex-husband was both violent and an ex. The man he found her in bed with seems to have run off without his trousers and out of her life. The co-habitee now cohabits with another woman, and the married man – whoever he was – appears to have remained married. So what Sharon lacked in quality she made up for in quantity.'

Colclough made a face.

'The psychologist feels our killer is probably someone who selects lonely woman – single, divorcees, separated . . . the women who are lonely, have children, little money and spend their time dreaming romantic dreams of Prince Charming. From what Sharon's friend says, she was like this. And judging from the statements, so was Stacey Farmer.

'The psychologist believes our killer is someone who has a distinct grudge against this type of woman. He suggested the killer might himself have been cheated on or jilted by a woman like this and it's his way of hitting back, at women in general but women like this in particular. So he made contact with them through the personal columns. And my belief is that when he turned up at the Quiet Woman on Tuesday night Sharon Priest had a bit of a shock. Because the man who invited her into his car posing as her Prince Charming was not some handsome stranger, as she had fondly imagined, but someone she already knew.'

She paused. 'The psychologists have always talked about the growing conceit of a serial killer,' she said. 'They claim as he gets away with crimes he gets braver. His crimes become more audacious and he kills on his own back doorstep. Perhaps Sharon was the one he meant to get in the first place and the other was a practice run . . .'

'So Piercy.' Arthur Colclough looked unconvinced. 'Where are you going to start?'

'Well,' she said cautiously. 'Sharon's shoe is still missing.' Again she gazed at the computer screen. 'No hint of that before,' she said. 'He didn't take a souvenir of his crime before.' She looked at Superintendent Colclough. 'The shoe must be somewhere. It can't have disappeared into thin air.'

'And it isn't on the moors,' Mike said. 'We've had a thorough search. It isn't there.'

'It may be a clue,' she said dubiously. 'I'm not absolutely sure. I suppose it could have been a trophy. What would be really lucky is if our killer doesn't know the shoe is missing. It could have fallen off in his car or somewhere.'

Colcough breathed out very hard in a slow whistle. 'Bit of a long shot,' he said.

Mike and Joanna nodded in agreement.

'Well, Piercy,' he said, slapping her on the back.

'This gives us plenty of work.' He paused for a moment, thinking, then asked about the wire.

'The cable, sir?' Joanna frowned. 'It's annoying me,' she said, pursing her lips thoughtfully. 'I feel I should recognize it. It's a thin, twisted steel cable. We've started enquiries around car shops, garages and so on, but we've got nowhere yet. It doesn't seem to fit into anything specific. Apparently it's too thin for car cable but we can't work out another use.'

'I wondered whether Macclesfield might lend us a couple of officers,' she said. 'It would give us a bit of a start. And after all, this might help clear up their unsolved murder too.'

It was much later and they were sitting in Colclough's office eating greasy chip-shop chips and drinking lager out of cans.

'It's funny,' said Joanna. 'Sharon had close friends but kept a lot of secrets from them.' She paused. 'I suppose somewhere near the top of the list of suspects has to be Finnigan, her ex-husband and father of the two older children. And he does have a history of violence.'

'Not sex attacks, though,' Mike pointed out. 'Not rape.'

'ABH,' she said. 'He knocked her about and broke her jaw.'

Arthur Colclough raised his eyebrows. 'I'm surprised he didn't get GBH for that one.'

'The old provocation card was flashed,' Joanna said.

'He did come home from night duty to find her in bed with another man.'

Colclough nodded. 'Did they get a divorce?'

'Yes, two years ago.'

'Then she took up with Paul Agnew,' Mike put in. 'He works at the oatcake shop at the top end of town.'

Joanna was in the act of sliding a chip into her mouth. 'Mike,' she said. 'We haven't asked anyone whether she had a job.'

'She had three kids,' Mike said. 'She wouldn't have had the time.'

'Part time?' Joanna said. 'It's worth a try.'

Mike nodded.

'I'll ask Christine tomorrow.'

Colclough was enjoying the chips too much to feel even a twinge of guilt. This felt like old times before he was too senior to enjoy a newspaper full of chips at the station. 'Nectar,' he said, puzzling the others. 'What was that you said about the father of the third child?'

'Yet another of the many mysteries of Sharon Priest's overcrowded sex life,' said Joanna. 'But he's almost certainly the married lover.'

'And we know nothing about him . . .'

Mike shrugged. 'No,' he said.

Colclough dabbled a chip on the sprinkling of salt. 'But somebody knows,' he said. 'And if he was married and she threatened to pull the plug on him it would give him an excellent motive for wanting her silenced.'

Joanna nodded. 'We'd thought of that,' she said, then glanced at the computer. 'But doesn't this look a little larger than a simple domestic affair?'

The Super frowned at her. 'Do we know nothing about this married man?'

'Bugger all,' Mike said gloomily, 'apart from the fact that he drives a smart car.'

Colclough popped the last of his chips into his mouth and stared at the greasy paper regretfully.

'Well, that really narrows the field,' he said. 'And the ad in the paper?' He was looking at Mike.

'Not much help,' Mike said gloomily. 'It seems they just hand over all the mail addressed to a particular box number. Anyone could have picked it up. It's really lax,' he grumbled. 'It could be anyone . . . The editor said half of the men who reply to the lonely hearts are married anyway.'

'So it doesn't even rule out married men.'

'Quite honestly, sir,' Mike said reluctantly, 'I don't think we'll ever know who all of them are.'

'Well, we don't need to know all of them, Sergeant,' Colclough said sharply. 'Just the one.'

Mike flushed.

The Super glanced at Joanna. 'You've got your work cut out, Piercy.'

She nodded. 'I know, sir.'

He grinned. 'You'll get there, in the end. But it'll take an awful lot of leg work.'

She looked at him. 'I've got to get him,' she said, 'otherwise he'll kill again.'

Chapter Seven

The day beckoned grey, cold and uninviting as Joanna drew back the curtains the next morning, but as she showered she felt exhilarated at the thought of the ride ahead and began to plan her day. It was time to meet Doreen Priest, Sharon's mother, but the prospect depressed her. The uniformed boys had informed Mrs Priest of her daughter's death and told her she would be interviewed later, but Joanna always found it hard – expressing sorrow and at the same time relentlessly pumping out the information she really needed, the less savoury details of a person's life. And she needed to talk to Christine Rattle again. There were so many unanswered questions. How many of them was she able to answer? Who was the man Sam Finnigan had found his wife in bed with? How had Paul Agnew been so sure Ryan had not been his son? Who was the unknown married man and why had they parted so acrimoniously? Had his wife known of his infidelities? Had she cared?

She squeezed a couple of oranges into a glass, switched the kettle on, then prepared some ground coffee. Years ago her mother had taught her to savour the food she ate. She poured out a dish of cereal and took the tray into the dining room so she could watch the birds fight over the mesh stocking of peanuts. But her mind kept pondering the case. And as she sat and ate her breakfast she had the distinct feeling that some of her questions would never be answered and a few of Sharon Priest's secrets would lie with her in her grave. When she got there. Permission for burial might not be released for several weeks yet.

She drank her coffee thoughtfully. And now there was this other murder. Would it further complicate the case or help solve it? She would have to speak to the Macclesfield investigating officers. And there was something else lying at the back of her mind, nagging away like a toothache. The wire cable twisted round the girl's neck until it bit her flesh and extinguished her life. Twisted, slim steel cable that reminded her vaguely of something . . . and she couldn't think what. Perhaps at the morning briefing some bright spark might enlighten her.

And then there was the suggestion she had made last night to the Super – that the killer came from Leek. Had he?

But if he hadn't, how had he known things about Sharon? How had he known she would look good in red? Had he a fondness for red and had merely said it without knowing?

But he knew her name. He knew the car she drove.

Joanna shook her head. He had to have been known to her. She must interview Christine again.

She stepped outside into the morning drizzle and watched the mist rising over the silent canal.

She was still frowning as she wheeled her bike out of the garage.

For the first fifty yards she felt cold on the bike, chilled by the wind, her legs stiff and tired from her car-driving days, and she wondered why the hell she bothered to cycle at all. Then the strength seemed to warm and invigorate her, make her legs quick and strong and she began to pedal to a hidden rhythm, humming as she moved.

'Hi.' It was Stuart drawing alongside her, white teeth flashing.

She grinned back at him, the pleasure of being on her bike making her suddenly happy. The day promised well.

He watched her critically as she pedalled up the hill. 'You're not doing badly, though.'

She felt hugely pleased at the compliment and they were silent companions until they reached the hill and the cars pulled past.

Stuart gave the drivers a sour look. 'The traffic's been awful the last couple of mornings.' He winked. 'Traffic lights on the main Cheddleton road. Lorries like a wall.'

She laughed and they shared the easy companionship of two people who enjoy the fresh air, the exercise, the challenge of a steep hill, not people who took the easy way. She watched with pleasure his feet flashing up and down, the slim figure bent low over the handlebars. He was fit. She had real trouble keeping up with him and after a minute or two she started panting.

'Whew,' she said as they neared the top of the hill. 'I'm sure this hill's getting both longer and steeper.'

'Bend down a bit lower,' he suggested.

'Can't. It knackers my back.'

He laughed. 'You'll soon get used to it. Just keep trying.'

'I do,' she said and she felt envious of the slim form, his strong legs, the seemingly effortless ride.

As soon as the road flattened out she felt a surge of energy.

'Great,' he said. 'Well done.'

They pedalled a bit quicker and were soon at the point where Joanna turned off. She raised her hand and waved. 'Bye, Stuart. I'll see you again, I expect.'

He grinned and carried on along the road and she turned into the station car park and locked her bike to the railings.

Mike was waiting for her in her office, a sheaf of papers in his hand. 'Can I speak to you before the briefing?'

'What is it, Mike?' She sat down.

He stared at her, his face pale and tense. 'It's these letters,' he said.

Her pulse quickened. 'What about them?'

'Prince Charming to Cinderella,' he said, sinking down into the chair. 'How can she have been such a fool?'

'Sorry?'

'Joanna, just listen to a few sentences. "Do you ever wonder why I love the colour red?" '

She frowned. 'Nothing in that.'

' "My dreams of you are in red because to me it is

a special colour. Blood, wine, roses." ' Mike jabbed the word with his finger. 'Blood, Joanna.'

'She might not have read anything into that.'

He picked up another letter. 'Then what about this? "Sometimes I dream I am making love to you." '

'Nothing in that either.'

Mike didn't even look at her as he read out the next sentence. ' "Until you beg me to stop." '

She was alerted now, like a hound with the scent of quarry in its nostrils. 'Go on.'

' "But, Sharon, my little bird," ' he quoted, ' "I won't stop. And in the end what I desire you will want too. I promise." '

'Are they all like that?'

Mike could hardly look at her. 'They're all the same, Jo.'

'All on the edge of perversion.'

She sat, silently pondering, then looked at him. 'Any fingerprints?'

He shook his head. 'Anyone with the IQ of a gnat would know to wear gloves but we'll get them checked out anyway.'

She shuddered. 'They're horrible, Mike.'

'But what beats me is why did she go out with him? It's obvious the guy was a complete pervert. Why the hell did she go?' His face took on a puzzled look. 'Any woman – surely – would smell a rat at this sort of stuff.' He slapped the letters down on her desk. 'So *why*?'

'I think,' she said slowly, 'I can answer that one. Christine said above all Sharon dreamed of excitement.'

'But surely . . .'

'No woman thinks she'll be harmed. They all dream of taming a stranger.'

'God,' Mike said disgustedly. 'What fools women can be.'

'And what . . .'

'Yes – all right.'

They stared at one another, both disturbed by the contents of the letters.

It was Joanna who moved first. 'I'd better get on with the briefing,' she said.

She began with the map pinned up on the board and a resumé of the case. Then she gave a brief description of the Macclesfield murder.

It was Timmis who picked up the point. 'Are we sure they're connected?'

'The MO is exactly the same,' Joanna said. 'It's too much of a coincidence that there should be two such similar murders a few miles apart. However, we're doing tests at the lab and the Cheshire Police should give us more info. We'll know more later on today. I'll keep you informed at tonight's briefing. The DNA tests, as you know, can take a while. For now,' she said, 'I want you to treat this as a routine murder hunt. In other words, focus your questioning on Sharon Priest's life and death. But . . .' She glanced around the room, 'if Stacey Farmer's murder is connected, I'm sure you realize, it's quite a man-hunt.'

There was a ripple of subdued comments. Everyone was watching her.

'According to the criminal psychologist we're probably looking at a man in his mid-twenties to thirties.

Someone who was dominated by his mother in his formative years.'

The murmurs grew louder and she caught one or two of the uniformed boys glancing at each other with a look of sceptical amusement. She knew they mistrusted her reliance on science. Leg work would be what solved this case. And not some bloody trick cyclist sitting in his ivory tower . . .

She smiled. No matter how many times psychologists were proved right, some of these officers would never be convinced. She ignored the murmurs and carried on reading out the psychologist's report.

' . . . then married and almost certainly divorced or separated. Possibly with children.'

A few of them groaned.

Timmis spoke. 'That describes half the male population of Leek,' he said gloomily. 'They're all married and divorced, separated, remarried, living in sin.'

'Yes, I know,' Joanna agreed. 'But it also describes two men we know who had recent, intimate relationships with Sharon. Sam Finnigan, her ex-husband. Thirty-seven years old, the father of two of her children, October and William. They were divorced two years ago. We know he is a violent man, that he was charged with ABH after he found her in bed with another man.' The wave of sympathy was tangible as it moved around the room.

'He broke her jaw,' she said sharply.

Mike, on her right, moved uncomfortably. 'Do we know who the other man was?'

She shook her head. 'No. But I want you to work

at finding out who he was, Mike. In other words, listen to the gossip.'

She turned her attention back to the roomful of police. 'Then her ex-boyfriend, Paul Agnew. He works at the oatcake shop in Pick Street. We don't know much about him except that he smokes grass. Supposedly he kicked her out just over a year ago when he found out she was pregnant.' She stopped. 'For some reason he refused to believe the child – Ryan – was his.'

A muttering moved around the room.

'Yes . . . yes,' she said impatiently. 'I've worked that one out too. But they were together less than a year. Unless he was impotent . . .'

All the males in the room shifted uncomfortably. This was a word that made them uneasy. Incest, murder, rape . . . These words they could cope with. But impotence . . .

'Well,' she said, 'this is something we need to find out, isn't it?' She faced them. 'Because if he was impotent he can't have bloody well raped her, can he?'

She turned back to the board and chalked up two more references. 'As well as those two suspects, according to her friend Christine Rattle Sharon had had an affair with a married man. We know very little about him except that she said he was "well off". Remember Sharon was barely financially solvent. Practically anyone with a Barclaycard and a bank account would have fitted the bill. So don't go hunting out all the local millionaires and accusing them.'

There was a ripple of laughter around the room.

'We don't know the name of this married man, but it seems they had some sort of a row. Christine

107

thought it was something to do with the baby who Christine believed was his son. Maybe he helped her financially with the child,' she said, recalling the expensive quilt on Ryan's cot.

She glanced at Mike, spoke in a soft aside. 'I'll ask Christine again about this guy.'

'Then there is the man who signed himself Prince Charming, the man we believe answered her ad in the personal column. Sharon's last date.' She blinked. According to Christine, he seemed to know things about Sharon that she definitely hadn't told him. She had all their attention now. 'I know,' she said. 'Explain that if you can. I can't, except by saying Prince Charming was someone who already knew his Cinderella.' Quickly she explained the reasons as she had discussed them with Colclough the night before.

'There is something else you should all know.' She glanced around the room. 'Prince Charming wrote Sharon several letters. Mike has been looking through them.' She paused. 'They show distinct evidence of perversion. This man is dangerous to women.'

She looked up. 'Any questions?'

'Have you any idea who Prince Charming is?'

'He could be anybody,' she said quietly. 'But I think it was the same Prince Charming who raped and garrotted Stacey Farmer in Macclesfield.'

'And you think he knew our girl, Sharon?'

Joanna perched on the corner of the desk and crossed her legs. 'As Colclough was warning me last night,' she said, 'we need to keep an open mind. But, as said, the modus operandi was exactly the same for both girls.' She paused. 'Both were picked up in a pub, as a result of lonely hearts ads. There were other similarities too. Stacey was a single-parent mum, desperate for romantic love, adventure . . . call it what you like. She was met at a pub by a man who would be difficult to recognize again – his anorak hood was turned up. He looked at no one, crossed the bar straight to her and they left together immediately. And she was raped, then garrotted. The killer used fine steel cable with part of a wooden broom handle to twist it.'

McBrine spoke up. 'Why?' he asked. 'Why use the broom handle?'

'Have any of you tried twisting cable?' she asked, her eyes sweeping the room.

No one had.

'To kill someone with wire as thin as that,' she said, 'would have cut our killer's hands. He needed to exert a certain amount of pressure. Therefore he used a broom handle.'

She glanced around the room. 'What I find most disgusting,' she said, 'is the fact that he preyed on two such needy and vulnerable women.' She paused. 'Both wanted to meet somebody who was kind to them – who cared for them – their idealized Prince Charming. And both were looking for excitement to light up their humdrum lives. Only in this case he wasn't exactly Prince Charming. More like Vlad the Impaler.

If he *is* the same man – and I think he is – he got away with killing Stacey. I don't want him to get away with it this time. And I don't want there ever to be a next time.'

There was silence in the room now. The gossiping and chatting that normally took place in the background of a briefing had died out as the officers chewed over her words.

Joanna stood in front of them and outlined her plans. 'DS Korpanski and I will speak to Sam Finnigan and Paul Agnew later on today, as well as Christine Rattle and Doreen Priest, Sharon's mother. Any questions?'

Timmis – always quick and vocal – objected. 'Can we rule anyone out?' He frowned. 'I mean a married man doesn't fit into the psychologist's profile, ma'am.'

'He could do,' she said slowly, 'if since the affair he split up acrimoniously from his wife. We don't know he's still married. He could be divorced. It is possible.' She felt she needed to concede a point. 'Anyway, we can't afford to exclude someone from the enquiries just because he doesn't fit into the profile.' She ignored the smirks and glanced at Mike.

'Tell them about the lonely hearts, Mike.' Gratefully she sat down.

Mike stood up, twisted the knot of his tie in embarrassment, cleared his throat. 'She had more than forty replies,' he said, then grinned. 'All those rampant men on the loose.'

'Just get on with it, Mike.' But the comment had sent ripples round the room and it was a minute or two before it was quiet again.

'I've managed to trace about half,' he said. 'Some of them were married, just after a bit on the side. One or two were positively weird. Not one admitted to actually having met up with Sharon. So many of the replies had no address—'

'They'll all have to be traced,' Joanna interrupted. 'Just in case they can tell us anything.'

Mike was fiddling with his tie. He cracked his knuckles and held up a sheet of paper. 'The letters from Prince Charming,' he said, 'were all handwritten. I've sent the originals off to forensics just in case they can turn up anything, but a sprinkling of magic dust only turned up smudged fingerprints. I think she'd handled them a lot.'

'We can live in hope,' she said. 'There's always ESDA – impression reading to you morons,' she said, laughing. 'But again, don't hold out too much hope. They'll also get the handwriting expert to take a look at them.'

Mike handed out a sheaf of paper. 'These are photocopies. See if you can find anyone who recognizes the writing.'

'It's a fairly distinctive hand,' Joanna said, glancing at one of Mike's copies.

WPC Sheila Locke spoke up. 'What about the postmark?' she asked shrewdly.

Mike made a face. 'No bloody envelope.'

As he cleared his throat and sat down, Joanna touched his shoulder briefly. 'Thanks,' she said.

Mike looked at her, his eyes gleaming. For a minute or two his gaze rested on her, but he said nothing more and she turned her attention back to the room.

'I don't suppose there's any lead on Cinderella's missing shoe?'

WPC Sheila Locke shook her head. 'I've found the shop where she bought them,' she said. 'They were brand new. She only bought them on Saturday, for a special date. The woman serving in the shop remembered Sharon. She said she seemed happy, lively and talkative and very friendly. And that's about it.' She looked at Joanna. 'Apart from that I've found out nothing. She was wearing them that night – both of them. One of them's disappeared. That's all.' After Mike's story she knew it was an anti-climax. 'I'm sorry,' she said and sat down.

Joanna looked at the knot of uniformed officers sitting halfway down the room on the right.

'What about the cable used to strangle her?'

'We've been everywhere – DIY, car shops, electrical retailers.' Greg Scott spoke up. 'We've got nowhere. It seems no one quite uses that particular cable in that thickness or that twist. Sorry.' He sat down.

'Don't worry,' she said, encouragingly. 'It's early days yet. We've got time.' But under her breath she added, 'I hope.'

Mike heard her, raised his eyebrows.

'Well,' she said softly, frowning at him, 'this is the second time – that we know of.'

He was staring at her. 'That we know of?'

'I've only looked at known murders,' she said. 'I haven't even touched the Missing Persons Files. And how many of those do you know are single, on the hunt for adventure and excitement – Deborah Halliday, just for one?'

He blinked. 'I hadn't thought of it,' he said.

She nodded. 'Exactly.'

*

The team who had started interviewing everyone who had been at the Quiet Woman that night were next to report.

DC Alan King stood up, an impressive figure, standing six and a half feet tall. 'Paul Agnew was at the Quiet Woman that night,' he blurted out.

'What?'

'The barmaid told us.' He leafed through his notebook.

'Was he there at the same time?'

'Apparently . . .' DC King was reading through the barmaid's statement. 'When she arrived he drained his glass and walked out without even looking at her. The barmaid knows Agnew by sight,' he added, 'but not Sharon.'

Joanna spoke quietly to Mike. 'Well, well,' she said. 'The worms are starting to crawl out of the woodwork.'

Mike nodded.

'Thanks, Alan,' Joanna said. 'Leave the statement on my desk. Well done,' she added. 'We'll have another briefing this evening, at six.'

The force dispersed.

When the room was empty Mike looked at her. 'Who shall we start with?'

'How about Doreen Priest?' Joanna said. 'I'm curious to know what she's like. And she might be able to enlighten us on a few points.'

Sharon's mother lived in a small terraced house on the extreme northern edge of Leek, one of the last houses in the town before entering Blackshaw Moor, the start of the long climb up to the Winking Man, the stone crag at the highest point of the road to Buxton. The garden was untidy, with plants dangling over the path and the lawn a mixture of mud, weeds and grass. The door was scratched at paw level. Joanna lifted the knocker.

It was opened by a short, stocky woman with straw-coloured hair wearing a dressing gown. She glared at Joanna. 'I was just going to bed,' she said in a voice gruff with too many cigarettes, and frankly hostile. But she didn't look distraught with grief.

'I'm Detective Inspector Piercy,' Joanna said, flashing her ID card. 'And this is Detective Sergeant Korpanski. We're investigating the death of your daughter.'

A quick spasm of pain flashed across the woman's face. She blinked and pressed back against the door. 'You'd better come in,' she said.

They followed her into a small, overheated room that stank of cigarettes. Doreen Priest switched the gas fire down.

'Cup of tea?' she asked.

Both Mike and Joanna nodded. This would not be a quick business.

Doreen Priest had put the three mugs on a plastic tray. 'I didn't know if you took sugar,' she said, handing round the bowl. Both declined and Doreen lit a cigarette.

'I always thought something might happen to Sharon,' she said. Then she looked purposely at Mike. 'You saw her. Good-looking girl, wasn't she?'

Mike nodded and Doreen took a long drag from her cigarette. 'Too bloody good-looking, that was her problem.' She waved her cigarette at him. 'Not that I'm saying she was a nympho. My Sharon wasn't like that. She was just a rotten picker. She got all the wrong men.' She gave a loud sniff and her breast heaved up and down quickly before she could speak. 'It's the kids I feel sorry for,' she said in a strangled tone. 'Them kids.'

'Mrs Priest,' Joanna said softly, 'were you on good terms with Sharon?'

Doreen crossed her short legs and considered. 'We used to be.'

'What happened?' Joanna leaned forwards.

Mrs Priest took another deep drag from her cigarette. 'Well, I didn't blame her for splitting up with Finnigan. He was a brute. I knew that when they got married. I did warn her. "Watch him, my girl," I said. "Watch him." ' Her small black eyes were bright as a robin's. ' "And watch him even more when he's a couple of pints inside him," I said. I was right. Though he weren't bad with October and William. Give him his due.' She stopped and gave a small laugh. 'But of course, you know Sharon . . .'

Neither Joanna nor Mike felt inclined to mention that, no, they did not know Sharon. Had not known Sharon. And now would never know Sharon.

Doreen carried on regardless. 'Anyway, Finnigan came home off nights – found her with this bloke.' She stopped. 'Something must have snapped. He nearly bloody killed her. Had to have her jaw wired straight.'

'Who was the man, Mrs Priest?' It was Mike who spoke.

They were due for a disappointment.

'Oh, just some bloke from work,' she said, airily dismissing him with a wave of her smoking hand. She sighed. 'Then she moved in with that nutcase, Agnew.'

She puffed twice on her cigarette before continuing her story. 'Well, I knew that was a waste of time. Never even got off the ground because he was always flippin' high as a kite. Besides,' She gave Joanna a bawdy wink, 'he had some very strange habits, that one. Personally me and Sharon thought he was pre-tty kinky. Then along comes this married man.' She stopped. 'And that was when I fell out with her. A married man, Sharon, I said. No way. I mean, I've got my bloody standards. And husband-sharing I do not approve of.'

Joanna squirmed.

'Who was the married man, Mrs Priest?' Mike spoke again.

An ugly, cunning look passed across the woman's face. 'I don't know,' she said, watching the tip of her cigarette glow. 'She never told me.'

Mike gave Joanna a swift glance.

'We sort of lost contact then,' Doreen said. 'I hadn't seen her since Ryan was born.'

'So you knew nothing about her plea for a Prince Charming?'

Doreen bit her lip. 'Not a thing,' she said. She waved her cigarette at them both. 'I'll do right by them kids. I'm telling you. I'll have October and Little Wills here. They can live with their gran. I love 'em,' she said defiantly.

'And Ryan?'

'Gran's' face was stony now. 'I'm not having that little bleeder here. He'll have to fend for 'imself.'

She watched them leave with a face still as hard as granite – unbending as far as Ryan was concerned.

'What's going on?' Joanna said to Mike. 'Ryan's her grandchild too. Why won't she take him?'

Mike shrugged. 'Leave it to the social workers, Jo,' he said, but she refused to be sidetracked.

'I'm just wondering whether her dislike of Ryan has any bearing on her daughter's murder.'

Mike made a face. 'How could it?'

'You tell me,' she said, 'but I intend keeping it in mind. Ryan's quite different from the other two. He's prettier, plumper. His clothes looked just a bit smarter. Even his cot cover. It looked more expensive.' She glanced at him. 'Surely you noticed?'

'Can't say I did,' he grunted.

'Well, I certainly did. He even sleeps with his mother.'

'He's the youngest.'

'And comes from a different stable,' she said decidedly.

Their car moved away from the small house and Joanna buckled her seat belt with a tinge of irritation.

'I thought we'd at least come away with some answers,' she grumbled. 'But we've gained nothing, just another question.'

She drew a lipstick across her mouth. 'Let's hope Christine Rattle's got a few answers. I'm a bit fed up with all these imponderables.'

She glanced at Mike. 'Drop me off, will you?'

'You don't want me to come?'

'I think she's more likely to talk to me alone than if you're there.'

He nodded. 'OK. I'll carry on back at the station till you're done. Read a few statements. Take another look through those letters.'

'We'll get the psychologist to study them.'

'You pay too much attention to psychology and not enough to traditional police methods.'

'I listen to both, Mike, but I can tell you, this killer has the *mind* of a killer. So it may well be that that traps him. Therefore we have to understand him.'

Mike grunted again and pressed the accelerator down hard.

Doreen Priest was watching as the police car drew away. She watched until it was out of sight and she felt sure they would not return. Then she drew her dressing gown tightly around her and sat with an unlit cigarette dangling from her mouth. She stared at the telephone for a long time before picking it up and dialling a number. She knew exactly what she would say. No need for open threats. She would simply point out that she was due for a very expensive time for the next few years if she was to bring up Sharon's children. No need to mention to anyone what she intended doing about Ryan. Early days yet. There was plenty of time.

*

The long curved stretch of council houses was deserted except for a few stray dogs wandering across the streets. One of them started barking as the car pulled up outside Christine Rattle's house.

Christine had made an attempt to make the house comfortable – luxurious, even. The lawn was neatly mown, weeds pulled up, the laburnum bush trimmed against the autumn.

Joanna pushed open the gate and walked up the path. Christine had been watching for her. She stood in the window, waved a half-smoked cigarette and met her at the door.

'I feel awful,' she said. 'Bloody awful.'

Joanna had no need to ask why.

'The kids.' Christine sank down on the sofa. 'What was I going to tell those poor kids? I kept saying, "Mummy'll come home soon." ' She gave a short laugh. 'Even bloody William didn't believe me in the end.'

Joanna gave an inadequate murmur, sat down on the sofa opposite Christine and accepted a mug of coffee.

'You can help us now,' she said, when Christine had come back from the kitchen. 'It'll help you, too – take away the feeling of guilt.' She knew she was supposed to offer counselling. But in her experience the guilt could be used to advantage in the investigation. Use vengeance in a constructive way because it was a potent energy source. So she prepared to spend as long as it took listening to Christine, whatever direction her thoughts took.

Christine gave a wry smile. 'I wasn't much bloody use to her, was I?' She closed her eyes wearily. 'You know, it was me what suggested she put that stinking advert in the paper?'

Joanna nodded.

'And it was probably him who killed her.'

'He could have known her anyway,' Joanna said cautiously.

'You think it's someone local?'

'At the moment we're working on that assumption.'

Christine took a long drag at the cigarette, seemed mesmerized at the bright red glow on the tip.

'Tell me,' said Joanna. 'What did Sharon think when one of the letters came back addressed in her name?'

'Bloody bowled over. Then she thought me or Andrea Farr, her pal at work, had let on to someone that it was her ad. You know.' Christine laughed. 'Sort of blind date, really.'

'And had you?'

'Well, I can't speak for Andrea,' Christine said, 'but I certainly didn't. Not a soul.'

'Did Sharon ever say anything about the . . . contents of the letters he wrote to her?' Joanna was watching Christine closely for a reaction.

'What do you mean?'

Joanna took a deep breath. 'Some of them were a bit suggestive.'

Christine seemed unmoved. 'Yeah, she told me sometimes he came over a bit . . . strong.'

'A bit *strong*?' Joanna frowned. 'It was more than that.'

Christine flicked the ash from the end of her cigarette and refused to meet Joanna's eye. 'I did warn her,' she said, and Joanna felt the vaguest tinge of disquiet. There was something strange in Christine's face – as if she were withholding something.

Joanna decided to change tack. 'Who was the man Finnigan found her in bed with?'

'Someone from her work, I think.' She stopped and thought. 'I never knew. She never told me.'

'Where did she work?'

'She was just a cleaner.' Christine rubbed her face with her hands.

'Where?'

'She used to do a couple of evenings at Blyton's Engineering.'

'And the man?'

'I don't know,' Christine said. 'I don't know. I don't think it was anyone serious. I mean, she'd been out with him once or twice. She took him back to her place.'

'And Finnigan caught them.'

For the first time in a couple of days, Christine laughed. 'The bloke – whoever it was – shot out leaving his trousers behind. Kept the street gossiping for days. You 'ave to laugh,' she said. 'They was livin' in the next street then. He threw her out. So she gets Jubilee Road. He loses his place and ends up in a flat.' She chuckled. 'Bloody lucky it wasn't the prison.'

She gave Joanna a quick look. 'He broke her jaw, you know. He was very violent . . . always threatenin' her and after that things got worse. Much worse. You know he hung the trousers out of the window.' She stopped. 'They were there for days. Poor old Sharon. She was too damned frightened to take them in again.

Anyway, after that Finnigan threw her out. Poor old Sharon,' she said again.' 'Never had much luck.'

'Had Finnigan been violent before?'

Christine thought for a moment before answering. 'Not so much violent,' she said slowly. 'More unpredictable.' She looked candidly at Joanna. 'Know what I mean? He'd lash out for nothing. Sometimes after he'd hit her she'd come round here and think about it. "What did I do?" she'd ask me. I couldn't tell her, could I?' Christine sighed. 'After that business with Sharon he changed. He'd always had a temper. But after that he got nasty, devious. He stopped going out so much, and when he did he'd get into fights and arguments, as though he had a grudge against . . .'

'Women?'

Christine nodded.

'And what about Agnew?' Joanna asked casually. 'What was he like?'

But she knew however carefully she worded these questions Christine was shrewd enough to guess exactly where they led.

'A bloody waster.' Christine was not going to mince words. 'You obviously haven't met Paul, have you? No, there's no need for me to tell you about him. Go and see him yourself. But I warn you, he's a very peculiar person.'

'He was at the pub the same night that Sharon was killed,' Joanna said.

'He was?' She looked up.

'Yes.'

'Mind you . . .' She bit her lip. 'There's one thing about Paul. He's in a world of his own most of the time. You never know with him what he's thinking. He dreams and then says such weird things.' She watched Joanna. 'It's possible he was at the pub and so was Sharon and he never saw her. He's spaced out – when he's got the money.'

Unexpectedly tears started into her eyes. 'You don't think it was him, do you? I wouldn't like to think it was Paul.' She leaned forward and spoke earnestly. 'You see, he isn't like Finnigan. I mean, Finnigan's violent – nasty. I can picture him batterin' Sharon to death. But she wouldn't have met him at the pub and gone off with him somewhere. She knew what he was like. And Paul, well, I know to you he's a lawbreaker, but there's no harm in him. He just dreams.' She paused. 'You know, he used to live across the road, with her. When she was pregnant – showing – you know – about four months he just told her to get out. I found out he was living with this girl and went round for Sharon to ask him why. He just laughed, said the baby made it difficult for him to stay.'

'That doesn't necessarily mean it wasn't his baby,' Joanna pointed out.

'Sharon had already told me he wasn't the father.'

'Where is Agnew now?'

'Still with Leanne.' Joanna paused for a moment, frowning.

'Leanne Ferry,' Christine said helpfully.

That name. She had heard it somewhere before.

'Christine.' She put her cup down on the flimsy wine table. 'How did Agnew know Ryan wasn't his baby?'

Christine stared for a moment out of the window before answering. 'You'll have to ask him that,' she said.

'Didn't Sharon ever tell you?'

Christine shook her head.

And now Joanna had stopped believing her. She paused for a moment before speaking again. 'What about the married man?' she said. 'The one she had an affair with?'

'I don't know . . .'

'Just tell me what you do know,' Joanna said. 'It doesn't matter if it seems unimportant. Anything.'

'I don't know who he was.' Christine looked around the room. 'I only know bits about him. You know, odd things she told me. I know he was rich. And I know he was married. And I know he gave her money for Ryan.' She stared at the police woman. 'Honest, Joanna, that's all I know about him. Sharon could keep her cards close to her chest when she wanted. She never let out a beep. It was only when I asked her outright who Ryan's dad was that she told me that much.'

'The money he gave her,' Joanna said. 'Was it a cheque or cash?'

'In notes. I saw it. She'd been out with him not long before Ryan was born. And he gave her the money. She showed it to me.'

'How much?'

'Four hundred pounds,' Christine said. 'In fifty-pound notes.'

'And after Ryan was born? Did he give more?'

'I don't know . . . honest.' Christine flushed. 'I never

124

asked her. They had a big row when Ryan was a few weeks old.'

'What about?' Joanna said quickly.

'About Ryan.'

'What *about* Ryan?'

Christine's face collapsed. 'I think he wanted him.'

Joanna stared at her. 'What?'

'Well, Sharon just said she felt used.' She stopped. 'I took it to mean he wanted Ryan.'

Chapter Eight

The shoe had become an object of fascination to him. He would take it out of the box, unbutton his shirt, cradle it against his naked chest, press the long, slim heel hard against him, feeling the prick of the point. Then he would finger the sharp toe. When he closed his eyes he could imagine the long, shapely leg leading up from the shoe to its dark junction. Sometimes he dressed the legs in the current shades of stocking, in Monsoon or Desert Sand, Tornado or Sirocco. Usually he chose Sirocco, a dark, mahogany colour that reminded him of black girls' legs.

And the diamanté bow flashed at him, winked at him with a titillating knowledge. But his fetish for the shoe was a dangerous fascination. Because if Lizzie ever found it there would be hell to pay.

After last time she had sworn there would be no more. No more giggling girls on the end of the telephone. No more 'staying overnight on business'. No more nights when her husband arrived home stinking of cheap scent. No more disgusting discoveries in the car.

Never again, she had said. And this time he really believed she meant it.

So he packed the box away at the back of the garage on the top shelf of a little tin cupboard. But simply knowing it was hidden away, waiting for him, was enough to stir him, knowing it waited – like him – for a safe opportunity.

Was any opportunity ever safe? Never mind. It waited and winked when he brought it out into the light. And it gave him quiet satisfaction from inside its box. But when Lizzie was visiting her mother. That would be when the fun began.

Joanna decided it was now time to meet the chief protagonists in this tragedy. She had learned about them from Sharon's best friend and from her mother. It was time to fix her own opinions. She and Mike decided they should first descend on Paul Agnew.

The oatcake shop had a grubby, modest and unattractive exterior, flaking sky-blue paint and steamy windows. They sat in the car, watching the two assistants through the window – the scruffy, slim man with straggling hair and the plump blonde girl.

Joanna glanced at Mike. 'Ready?'

He nodded.

She already felt she knew Paul Agnew. Christine had done a good job describing him. As she and Mike squeezed into the small, stuffy shop with its scent of cheese and warm cooking oil he looked up and met her eyes. For a brief moment he stared at her. Then he broke his stare, wiped his sweating face with the back of his hand and looked away, down at the floor.

They waited their turn, watching the girl tip the

mixture on the griddle, wait for a moment before neatly flipping the pancakes over. Then it was their turn and Agnew was staring at Joanna again.

'Paul Agnew?' she said steadily.

He looked up, nodded.

'We want a word with you.' Mike could never quite keep the aggression out of his voice. Result: already Agnew looked threatened.

'Is it about . . .?' For comfort he looked at Joanna. She nodded.

Agnew turned to the girl at his side. She smiled sympathetically, gave the two police officers a look of dislike, jerked her thumb towards the door beyond.

They followed Agnew in.

It was a store room. Flour and milk, two big plastic bottles of oil. There was nowhere to sit and it was dark.

Agnew stood in the corner, like a boxer facing his opponent.

'I'm Detective Inspector Piercy,' Joanna began. 'This is Detective Sergeant Korpanski. We're investigating the murder of Sharon Priest.'

Agnew's eyes flipped from one to the other.

'Tell me about her,' Joanna said.

He shrugged. 'What do you want to know?' he asked stiffly. 'There ain't a lot to tell really. We was livin' together, but not for long. She was all right. We got on OK. No great problems.'

'You were fond of her?' Mike's voice was gruff.

'Yeah,' Agnew said hesitantly. 'I was. I was fond of 'er. She was a nice bird. A decent bird.'

Joanna felt her hackles begin to rise at his words. She took in a deep breath. Mike grinned across at her and she knew he would pull her leg about this when they had left the shop.

'For how long did you live with her?'

'Few months. I don't know exactly.'

'Did you get on well with the kids?'

He looked surprised at that. 'Yeah,' he said again. 'They was nice kids. I did like 'em.' He stopped and thought. 'They was OK.'

'So you like kids, Paul?'

He shuffled his feet. 'Yeah.'

'So why did you throw her out when she got pregnant?'

Agnew looked around the room like a trapped animal.

'She was pregnant, Paul,' Joanna said. 'Was the baby yours?'

Agnew stared at the floor and shook his head.

'It wasn't?'

Again he shook his head. 'Nope.'

'How did you know it wasn't?'

Agnew's face seemed to change. A look of cunning crossed it, then he took a step towards Joanna. And although Mike was there she felt the faintest pricking of fear.

'I got my tastes,' Agnew said, and she smelt the sweet tang of marijuana on his breath. 'I likes certain things.' He stared at Joanna. And this time it was she who broke the gaze. '*Different* things,' he said and swallowed.

'Put it like this. She weren't co-operative.' He swallowed again. 'That's how I knew. The kid weren't mine. Understand?'

Joanna glanced at Mike. He was glaring at Agnew as though he could throttle him. 'So if it wasn't yours, Agnew,' Mike said, 'whose was it?'

For the first time Agnew looked angry. 'You bloody well tell me that,' he said. 'You're the fucking detectives. All I know is that it weren't my kid.' He stopped. 'So I left.'

'Just like that?' Even to Joanna's ears Mike sounded disbelieving.

'Yeah,' he said. 'Just like that. I aren't like Finnigan. Brutality isn't my scene. As I said, I got other tastes. I weren't going to stand by and watch her swell up with a kid I knew weren't mine. But neither was I going to rough her up. She is a bird,' he said, then glanced at Joanna. 'Was. I weren't happy about the kid. So I left her to it.'

'Did you harbour a grudge?'

Agnew turned to Joanna. 'No,' he said. 'Not really. I sort of felt sorry for her.'

Joanna nodded. 'Some men,' she said softly, 'might have been angry with Sharon for going off with someone else.'

'Not me,' he said shortly. 'I had an idea why she went. In a way I didn't blame her. Me and her was different.' He grinned. 'Sexually. So we parted.'

Mike took a step forward. 'Where were you Tuesday night, Agnew?'

He blinked. 'I can't remember. You'll 'ave to ask my bird.' He leered at Joanna. 'She'll know. Like a walking bloody diary, Leanne is.'

'You wouldn't have been in the Quiet Woman on Tuesday night, would you?' she asked quietly.

He shrugged. 'Don't know. Might have been.'

'We have witnesses,' Mike broke in, 'who say you were in the Quiet Woman. Did you see Sharon there?'

Agnew frowned. 'Don't remember.'

'Had you arranged to meet her there?'

Agnew gave her the full force of his disconcerting stare. 'I haven't arranged to meet Sharon since we split,' he said. 'And definitely not in the last couple of months. Look . . .' He approached Joanna again. 'We finished – completely – about a year ago. If someone says she was there and I was there at the same time they might be right. I can't say.' The scent of unwashed feet and armpits was strong in the small room. 'I didn't see her. And that's what I'm tellin' you. All right? Anyway,' he added, 'I've found myself another bird now – better. I don't remember seeing her.' He grinned. 'I wasn't in much of a noticing mood.'

'Too much dope?' Mike asked.

Agnew looked sulky.

Mike pressed the point home. 'Sure you didn't follow her out of the pub on Tuesday night?'

Agnew shifted nervously. 'No,' he said. 'I didn't. I went straight home to me new bird.'

'And smoked another joint?' Mike stood over him like a Goliath. 'I thought you couldn't remember.'

'I'm just guessing. Look, I honestly couldn't give a monkey's arse for Sharon no more. She's history, my friend. History.'

He stopped for a minute, swallowed hard, his Adam's apple bobbing up and down in his throat. 'If you want to find out about Sharon – who got her that night – you want to find out who the bloke was who saddled her with Ryan. He was married. He would have a much better reason than me for wanting her out of the way.'

'So who was he?' Mike was almost shouting.

'I don't bloody know,' Agnew said hopelessly. 'I don't. I've thought about it. Perhaps it was someone she worked with. I don't know.'

'She must have said something?'

'She didn't.' He paused. 'She couldn't half keep a secret, Sharon.'

It was the first complimentary comment he had made about her.

Joanna was watching him carefully. 'Do you care that she's dead?'

He looked uncomfortable. 'Yeah – of course . . .'

'OK, Agnew,' Joanna resigned herself to getting nothing more out of him. 'That's all – for now.'

She was glad to leave the shop.

As she had expected, Mike turned to her in the car, a mischievous grin on his face. 'Quite a description, that.' He stopped. 'What did he say now? "A nice bird." "A decent bird." ' He gave a quiet chuckle. 'Describes quite a few women.'

She met his eye in the car mirror, laughed too.

'It made me wince,' she said.

'I could see that. You looked as though you'd sucked a lemon then had a mouthful of chilli pepper.'

She laughed again. 'Quite a description, Mike. But,' she warned, 'no leg pulls back at the station, please. Sharon may well have fitted the description of a "nice bird". I can tell you. I would not find the description flattering.'

'No,' he agreed with a wry smile. 'I don't suppose you would.' His eyes were still on her.

She started the engine. 'Now for Finnigan,' she said with a sigh.

But her private thoughts were mulling over what Paul Agnew had said: how had men viewed Sharon Priest? As a nice bird. A decent bird. One who could keep a secret well. Certainly her relationships had consistently broken up because she had met someone else. Finnigan had found her in bed with another man. While living God knows what kind of life with Paul Agnew she had become pregnant. She had had an affair with a married man . . . someone rich. Had Sharon been a woman easily bored by comfortable, domestic relationships, always craving excitement? Could that have been the stimulus of the letters, the lure to her last, dangerous assignation?

Joanna frowned and caught sight of herself in the mirror.

And how had women viewed Sharon? Certainly Christine Rattle had been fond of her – admired her – seen her as a loyal friend, a good mother, a young woman who had wanted her youth, to have a good time.

She compared this with the picture she herself had formed of her.

A young woman – quite slim, although her body showed obvious signs of childbearing. Empty breasts with stretch marks silvering pale flesh.

Probably she had been pretty in her cheap, stretch clothes. Diamanté flashing an invitation.

She turned to Mike. 'Describe Sharon,' she said.

He started with her observations. 'Slim, probably pretty in a cheap way. Dyed hair. A lot of make-up.' But then his view became more definitely masculine. 'I expect she was full of the old "come on",' he said. 'Probably a bit of a tease. Sexy, a bit tarty.' He grinned. 'I bet she was good fun, though. The sort of girl that would make a party move.'

She smiled at him. 'Thank you, Mike,' she said, then sighed. 'And now I suppose we'd better tackle Finnigan.'

Sam Finnigan was to be found on the top floor of a large Victorian house now divided up into flats. The front garden was weed-smothered, the gate missing. Only the hinges were left to rust. The path was slippery with leaves fallen from the roadside tree. The stone steps leading up to the front door were worn and the porch was lined with chipped tiles.

Mike pushed open the front door. The spacious hall was empty and had a cold, unwashed look, cobwebby and dusty. The smell of stale, rancid fat, old fish and chips mingled with recently applied vinegar.

Varying beats of pop music wafted down the stairs, punctuated by the sad cadence of a violin. Someone in the flats liked classical music.

Joanna glanced at Mike and the two of them ascended to the first-floor landing, passing a window of frosted glass behind which they could see the vague shape of a man urinating. They heard the sound of an old-fashioned flush and then the man emerged. Dirty, unwashed, unshaven. Bleary-eyed, he blinked at the two police officers as though they were offerings from outer space.

'Mr Finnigan?' Joanna asked tentatively.

The man looked her up and down in an appraising way, then jerked his thumb heavenwards. 'Top floor, my love,' he said, zipping up his flies and pushing past them.

She caught the waft of stale beer on his breath, rolled her eyes at Mike and they clattered up to the top floor.

Two doors faced them, both wearing chipped, brown paint. Joanna instinctively chose the one with the smashed-in panel, and knocked hard enough to tell Finnigan that this was an official visit.

The door opened to reveal another grubby T-shirt half covering a swollen beer belly, more stale beer breath, unshaven face and bleary eyes.

'Mr Finnigan?' she said again and he nodded.

'The law?' he asked.

'That's right.' She flashed her ID card at him. 'I'm Detective Inspector Piercy. This is Detective Sergeant Korpanski. We're investigating the murder of your ex-wife, Sharon Priest.'

Sam Finnigan scratched his head. 'I thought you'd get here sooner or later,' he said. 'I suppose Rattle's been rattling.'

His eyes suddenly brightened and he gave a loud guffaw at his own wit.

Neither Joanna nor Mike smiled.

'She *was* your wife, Mr Finnigan,' Joanna said pointedly.

For one short moment Sam Finnigan looked stung. He took a few deep breaths, glared at the two police officers, then stood back. 'I suppose you'll have to come in.'

They followed him into a large room strewn with dirty clothes and empty lager cans. A blanket was rumpled on the sofa, which Joanna guessed doubled as a bed. The atmosphere was stale.

Finnigan picked up a couple of token socks, then, finding nowhere to put them, dropped them in the corner. 'Sorry,' he said, 'bit of a tip. Didn't expect visitors,' he added nastily.

Joanna and Mike cleared a space, sat down and faced him.

'Look,' Finnigan said. 'Just because I bloody hit her once it doesn't mean I killed her.'

'I believe you hit her more than once,' Joanna said coolly.

Finnigan glared at her. 'Once on record, and she fucking well asked for it. Not that I expect either of you two to bother believing me.'

Joanna leaned forward. 'It's our job, especially in a murder case, to question everything anyone says to us. Especially ex-husbands. Especially ex-husbands who have a record of violence towards the deceased.'

Finnigan looked as though he was going to hit her. 'Give a dog a bad name.'

'Nobody's accusing you, Finnigan.' Mike's tone was saracastic. 'Yet.'

Finnigan had obviously met his type before. He stared at Mike, his face twisted with dislike. 'Don't get fucking smart with me, copper,' he snarled. 'You won't be able to pin anything on me. I'm clean.'

He gave Joanna a hard, defiant look. 'Clean as a baby's bottom,' he said.

'I'm sure . . .' Joanna spoke calmly and very politely. *Keep the heat out of situations.* It was Colclough's war cry. *Don't introduce aggression. There'll be plenty on the other side.*

Joanna cleared her throat. 'Just start at the beginning, Mr Finnigan.'

His gaze rested on Joanna. 'What do you want to know?' He frowned in a fuddled confusion. 'Do I need my solicitor here?'

'Not yet,' Mike said.

'Just tell me about Sharon.'

'What?'

'What was she like?'

'Sexy . . .' Finnigan grinned and Joanna felt herself flush. 'Bloody good in bed. That was the trouble. You see, men liked her. She was a randy bitch. Hot.' He gave a lascivious grin. 'Know what I mean, Detective Inspector?'

'I might remind you, Finnigan,' she said, dropping the title, 'Sharon is dead. Her children – and yours too – are in care.'

'Yeah, well, I can't 'ave 'em 'ere, can I?'

'That isn't the point,' Joanna said. 'She was murdered quite brutally after being raped. Please . . .'

Finnigan glowered. 'Look, she might be dead.' He sneered. 'It don't alter what she was. Bloody anybody's. Hot and wet with her legs always open and her knickers off. And there was plenty of takers. You asked me, copper. I'm just telling you. That's all.'

He stopped for a moment, then gave a soft burp,

crossed the room to a scratched chest of drawers. From the top he took a can of lager, burped again and snapped back the ringpull.

'Sorry I can't offer you one,' he said, leering. 'I can't go so far as to be hospitable. See?'

He took a long, calm drink, then sat down again can in hand. 'One thing about me,' he said. 'I can't pretend. I'm an honest Joe. I did knock her about a bit.'

Joanna nodded.

'I found her in bed with a bloke.'

She leaned forward. 'Who was he, Finnigan?'

He blinked. 'I thought you'd know,' he said.

'Who was he?'

'A good-looking guy. Sort of muscular.'

'Built like Mike here?'

Finnigan considered the Detective's burly frame, then shook his head. 'Sort of slimmer, but strong.' He peered into his can of beer. 'Bloody cow,' he said.

Joanna was beginning to feel disappointed. 'Don't you know any more about the man?' she asked. 'Didn't Sharon tell you who he was?'

Finnigan stood up, his face a picture of fury. 'It was fucking dark,' he said. 'Dark. Didn't Rattle tell you that? It was the middle of the fucking night. The light was off.' He stopped. 'I didn't want to wake the cow. I got in. Don't you thick coppers understand? I got into bed. And there was a bloke there.'

Even after years on the force Joanna was shocked. 'No,' she said softly. 'No one told me. I didn't know it was like that.'

Finnigan sat down heavily and some of the beer

slopped out of the can. 'I wish I'd 'ave killed her,' he said. 'She's deserved every single thing she's got.' He came to suddenly and focused on the two police officers. 'As I said, I'm an honest Joe.'

And for all the aggressive swagger, she felt some sympathy for the man. *All villains are like this –* another of Colclough's famous sayings – *usually stupid, mostly bad. But there's almost always something pitiable there.*

'If it's any help,' he said, 'I thought it was probably someone from where she worked. You know, Blyton's.'

Joanna nodded. 'Would you recognize him if you saw him again?'

'No, I don't think so.' Finnigan pondered the point for a moment. 'I ain't never seen him around Leek.'

'Did he speak? Did he have an accent?'

'Sort of made a noise,' Finnigan said. 'But he didn't speak. Just gave a shout. That's all.' He grinned. 'I think he shouted "Shit!" then he gave a funny kind of scream.'

Joanna sighed and took a swift glance at Mike. He was looking fed up. She had another thought. 'Well,' she said. 'If you didn't really notice him, did you see his car?'

'Nope. If I had I might have guessed something was going on. But I didn't see a car.' He thought for a moment. 'There weren't no car.'

'Might it have been parked round the corner?' Mike asked helpfully.

'There ain't a corner near the house,' he said, scowling. 'It's a long straight road. And there weren't no bloody cars.'

'He must have walked, then.'

'A neighbour?' Mike suggested.

'Don't be bloody daft,' Finnigan said. 'I knew everyone in the road. They wouldn't have gone with her. They'd have known what was coming to them if they had. I'd have bloody killed them. Besides, I'd have recognized a neighbour, wouldn't I?'

'Didn't anyone see the man running off?'

'It was three o'clock in the bloody morning.'

Mike was watching Finnigan suspiciously. 'If it was three in the morning, Finnigan, and you were supposed to be working all night,' he said, 'why did you come home?'

Finnigan shifted, uncomfortable. 'I thought something was going on,' he said.

'Why?'

Finnigan glared at her. 'Because she never felt like it,' he said. 'She was off sex. And that was like a pig going off its swill.'

Joanna tried another track. 'Since you split up,' she said, 'have you had much contact with Sharon?'

'Nah, court order,' he said. 'If I'd have seen her likely I'd have knocked her. Anyway, she kept out of my way.' He tried to take another swig out of the can, found it empty and stared miserably into it.

'And the children, October and William?'

Finnigan shook his head. 'Only with a social worker. Couple of hours a week.' He made a face. 'I'm no good with kids.'

Joanna crossed her legs, leaned back on the sofa, aware of lumps beneath the cushions. Lager cans?

'Where were you on Tuesday night, Mr Finnigan?'

He slewed a sideways glance at her. 'You sure I don't need my solicitor?' he asked suspiciously.

'Not yet,' Joanna said innocently. 'Now where were you the night she died?'

'Here,' Finnigan said. 'Watching telly. Drinking lager.' With sudden, shocking violence he crunched the can to an hourglass shape and hurled it across the room. It gave a hollow ping as it hit the side of the room and spat lager on to the yellowing wallpaper to join the random pattern of other dents and drips. 'Where the fuck do you think I go on a UB40? The fucking Ritz?'

Joanna felt oppressed and nauseated by the stuffy, smelly atmosphere, and was anxious to leave. But Mike's interest was aroused.

'Can you prove you were here all evening?' His voice was hard. Joanna knew his fists would be itching. Finnigan knew it too and eyed the Detective Sergeant uneasily. Slowly he shook his head.

Joanna moved to another area. 'Who was the married man Sharon had been seeing?'

Finnigan shook his head. 'I don't know,' he said. 'After my time, thank God. I heard she was seeing someone. I heard it was a rich guy, married. I said good luck to her. Of course,' he added cynically, 'he dropped her when Ryan was on the way.'

'How do you know that?'

'Rattle,' he said. 'She's a bugger for the gossip. Besides,' he added, 'why would she advertise if she wasn't short of a bloke?'

'You knew about the advert?'

141

He nodded. 'Cheap, weren't it? I never thought she'd stoop so low.'

Mike leaned forward. 'How did you know she had an advert in the paper?'

'I read it,' Finnigan said. 'It was bloody obvious it was her.'

'How?'

Finnigan thought. 'Well, she was always on about wanting a Prince Charming. Bloody obsessed. She fancied herself in red and was always saying she wanted a bit of sparkle. Know what I mean?'

'Are you saying anyone could have guessed it was Sharon who put that advert in?'

Finnigan shook his head. 'No,' he said. 'I ain't. I'm saying anyone who knew her well would know it was her.' He stopped for a minute. 'They would have to know her *well*.'

Joanna glanced at Mike and knew exactly what he was thinking. It was a long list.

Once back inside the police car Joanna glanced at her watch. 'Come on, Mike,' she said. 'There are a few things I want to do, and then I want to get the briefing over and done with and get home. I'm tired.' She yawned.

He raised his eyebrows. 'And I had you earmarked for a late night tonight.'

'I would do,' she said, 'but I really am knackered.' She grinned at him. 'It's a bath, a book and bed for me tonight.' She looked at him. 'Mike,' she said tentatively.

'How much do you think we should be looking at Stacey's murder rather than concentrating on Sharon?'

'I've glanced through the file,' he said. 'There doesn't seem anything particular to go on. No descriptions. No identity. Nothing.' He stopped.

'Perhaps they'll have the DNA test results at the hospital. I'll give Matthew a ring.'

Mike grimaced. 'I suppose they might.'

They were silent for a while, then Joanna spoke. 'Do you think it could have been someone who worked at Blyton's? Maybe the man Finnigan found her in bed with?'

'Well, someone will know,' he said. 'You know what gossips people in small firms are. Someone will know.'

And she was inclined to agree with him.

They had reached the station. She parked the car and switched off the engine, but neither of them moved.

'What if someone heard her talking about the advert,' Joanna mused, 'either at work or one of the men she had already been sleeping with? What if they decided to set her up, meet her, kill her?'

'There's so many possibilities,' Mike grumbled. 'It gives me a headache just thinking about it.'

'We'd better set up a line of enquiry at Blyton's?'

Mike nodded in agreement.

'Good.' She was satisfied. 'I have the feeling that Blyton's will bear fruit.'

'It had better,' Mike said soberly. 'Because Colclough's going to want results.'

*

143

The team was already assembled as she and Mike walked in. He sat beside her at the table.

So far the results of the investigations were disappointing. All the work – the interviews with everyone who had been at the pub that night, the combing of the moors, the examination of Sharon Priest's house, the studying of the remaining letters – had yielded disappointingly little.

No one had yet found the missing shoe. Still no one had tracked down the twisted steel cable used to kill her.

The assembled officers felt disheartened. Because they all knew he was out there. And now they were worried that they would fail and the killer of Stacey Farmer who had got away with it would also get away with murdering Sharon Priest.

Only Joanna, even at this early stage of the investigation, had not the slightest doubt that they would catch him. She stood up after listening to the various reports.

'Our next step,' she said, 'should be to scrutinize Blyton's, where Sharon Priest worked as a cleaner two evenings a week.' She nibbled her thumbnail.

'At the moment,' she continued, 'we know that our killer may have murdered before. We're waiting for DNA results which will confirm or deny this. It's possible he comes from Leek. It's also possible that he already knew Sharon Priest when he replied to her advert. According to Sam Finnigan, Sharon's ex-husband, anyone who knew Sharon reasonably well would have connected the lonely hearts ad with her. Certain typical phrases were used.

'We still don't know all of Sharon's men friends, notably the married man she had an affair with, the father of her youngest child, Ryan, and also the man she had an affair with while still married to Sam Finnigan, the man he found her in bed with.'

She turned to Mike and spoke to him. 'And I wouldn't mind betting someone tipped Finnigan off that his wife was having an affair. I expect they rang him that night at work.'

Mike's eyes gleamed and he nodded. 'I thought coming home at three in the morning was a bit strange.'

She turned her attention back to the room. 'Now, Sharon might have discussed the insertion of the advert with someone at work. That person might have leaked the information – perhaps unintentionally – or they might have been overheard.'

She smiled. 'Any questions?'

'Finnigan,' someone called. 'Is he clean?'

'He fits the psychologist's profile. He's quite bitter against Sharon, and even to us he didn't fake any real grief for her. But so far,' she said, 'he's clean. We've nothing on him.'

'And Agnew?' someone muttered. 'Pot-smoking little prat.'

'I don't know. There's something unsavoury about him.' She stopped. 'But as for being a killer – I don't know.'

'Yeah, but, ma'am.' PC Mark Timmis could be quite persistent at times. 'He was at the pub that night.'

'I know,' she said, 'but he's so fuddled with marijuana half the time I honestly don't know whether he even registered the fact that Sharon was in the Quiet

Woman at all. Agnew claims he spent the rest of the evening back at home with his new girlfriend, Leanne Ferry.' The name continued to buzz around at the back of her mind like a bloodthirsty mosquito . . .

Chapter Nine

She had barely turned out her bike on to the main road when Stuart shouted, 'Joanna!'

She slowed and waited for him to catch her up. He was panting hard. She raised her hand. 'Hi,' she said. 'Just finished work?'

Today he was fly-eyed in tinted goggles and crash helmet. And he was struggling to catch his breath. 'Don't usually see you on your way home.' He panted. 'Working late or finishing early?'

She grimaced. 'I seem to finish at a different time every day. I don't really work regular hours.'

They approached the brow of the hill. In front of them the temptation of swift descent. But the sudden blast of an easterly almost threw Joanna off balance.

'Traffic's easier today,' Stuart commented as they flew downwards.

'Yes,' she agreed.

But all descents come to an end and now there was the long hill to climb and a steady flow of traffic passing them.

An ambulance screamed behind them and instinctively they pulled in. Once stopped Stuart pushed his goggles up and blinked.

'Joanna,' he said shyly, 'do you mind if I ask you something?'

For some unknown reason she imagined it would be to do with her work. But it wasn't. And afterwards she realized he didn't even know she was in the police force.

'I wondered if you'd like to come out one night, for a drink?' He paused. 'Would you?'

Despite the cold her face felt hot. She didn't know what to say. Embarrassment was quickly replaced with anger with herself. For goodness' sake, Matthew was married. She might as well get on with her life solo. But she couldn't quite convince herself.

'Look,' she said, hesitating. 'I'm a bit tied up at work at the moment. I would like to – maybe in a week or two?'

He grinned and she had another glimpse of his beautiful teeth.

Joanna knew if she was to find any pleasure in life she must deny the spectre of Matthew which prevented her from forming other relationships. Even this vague arrangement with Stuart was making her feel marginally guilty as she pushed her feet back into the toe clips and sped along the flat.

Stuart soon caught up with her and handed her a slip of paper. 'Here's my telephone number. Just give me a buzz when you're free.'

She had trouble holding the paper between her thumb and finger. It threatened to blow away. Laughing, she tucked it in the back pocket of her cycling top.

Even beneath his Oakleys she could see he was

pleased. There was a change in the shape of his mouth, a satisfied tilt upwards.

She pedalled rhythmically to a pounding tone, reasoning with herself.

What about Matthew?

Why shouldn't I go out and enjoy myself? Stuart shot past her in a burst of energy and she continued her silent conversation. He's nice, he's pleasant. I bet he isn't married. I bet he doesn't have a daughter.

Stuart swerved out into the middle of the road in an exuberant, risky dance and, sharing his energy, she made a little bend too, a concession to having shed a small part of her load. Since her affair with Matthew she had led the life of a nun. Apart from Tom and Caro her life had been work, only work.

Already she was feeling lighter. Maybe she could shed the whole load. Maybe she didn't really need to carry the guilt around with her like a frame rucksack.

The arguments achieved something. She decided. If – she quickly replaced the 'if' with a 'when' – *when* they solved this case, she would enjoy a drink with him. Just a drink.

There was a note pushed under her front door and for a moment she caught her breath and thought it might be another threat from Jane. Then she recognized the writing. *I'm hoping you'll be home well before eight as I'm in a cooking frenzy. Beware the stomach!*

The signature was a flourished 'T'.

The scent of garlic wafted out of the doorway as she knocked to ask if she should bring red or white wine. Tom was dressed for the occasion in a navy and white striped butcher's apron. He grinned at her. 'Concoction *du cochon*,' he said and she laughed.

'Good, I'm starving.'

'Uuum – red,' he said before taking her elbow firmly and steering her out through the door. 'Now, you be a good girl. Have a shower and get dressed up. I promise it will be a meal . . .' he rolled his eyes, 'fit for a Detective Inspector.'

She laughed again and looked at him. His thin face was alight and warm. 'You're celebrating something,' she said.

Tom frowned, then exploded into laughter. 'Honestly, Jo, you're like a maiden aunt. I can't keep anything from you.'

'What is it?' she asked curiously.

'Oh . . . Nothing very much. Only – Caro has agreed to come on holiday with me next month.'

'Oh, Tom,' she said. 'I'm so happy for you.' And she kissed his cheek.

'It's such a small step,' he said. 'Three weeks. Not exactly a lifetime.'

'It's a giant step for you, though,' she said soberly.

But entering her own cottage she felt a sudden quick tinge of jealousy. No three-week holidays for her. At least – not with Matthew. And she kicked her shoes off so hard they bounced against the opposite wall.

'Damn,' she said, and felt evil.

She and Tom were best friends. She should feel happy for him. Not envious. And just to punish herself for being mean-spirited she turned the shower thermostat down to just above cool and forced her body to stay there for more than five minutes. But when she came out she felt a warm glow. Virtue and the relief of escaping the chilling gush. She wrapped a thick white towel around her and poured herself a glass of cold white wine from the fridge. She drank it thoughtfully. It was always the quiet minutes like these that she treasured. She switched the CD player on to some Mozart flute and harp music, closed her eyes and dreamed. It was what her mother used to call quality time.

It was her stomach rumbling that brought her back to the present. She dressed in blue silk shirt and black woollen leggings, pulled on some boots, sprayed herself with Ombre Rose, loving the strange, exotic smell of a spice market. She brushed her hair and creamed her skin. Applied mascara and a smear of lipstick. The nice thing about dinner with Tom was that he was far more absorbed in his culinary skills – or lack of them – than he was interested in his guest's appearance. And she knew from experience that if she questioned him tomorrow he would have no idea what she had worn.

She poured herself another half-glass of wine and by the time she turned up for the second time that evening on Tom's doorstep her mood had lightened.

Tom was an intriguing cook. Cooking relaxed him. He loved making weird concoctions, treating the kitchen as he would a chemist's laboratory suitable for experiments. He would always start off the same way – the way most cooks do – with a recipe book, a shopping list of ingredients, equipment. But that was where the similarity ended. He would then prowl the kitchen, grabbing bits and pieces, herbs and spices, throwing them in and treating himself to frequent tastings. He could never repeat a recipe. And sometimes Joanna was glad. There had been some memorable failures. Chicken when mixed with garlic, rice, lemons, olive oil and too many chillis had been mouth-burningly delicious. But fillet steak with nuts, digestive biscuits, tomatoes and breadcrumbs had been very difficult to swallow.

Still, at least he looked the part.

She pulled the cork from the bottle.

'It smells brilliant,' she said. 'And I'm starving.'

Tom observed her with a serious expression. He lifted the lids from the steaming saucepans.

She knew she was expected to gaze reverently inside.

It looked like pork in a creamy sauce. She sat down and waited.

'I've suddenly lost confidence.' He gave a twisted smile. 'I don't know what it'll taste like.'

'That's never stopped you before.'

He made a face, leaned across the table to poke a knife into the asparagus.

She picked up her wine glass. 'Well, the wine's fine,' she laughed.

He gave a sudden, mischievous grin. 'One way to get a drink,' he said. He ladled food on to plates and they sat down to eat.

She took a mouthful of the creamy meat. There was too much pepper in it.

He watched her. 'Sorry,' he said. 'I think sometimes

when I'm tasting I forget to stir it first. Then I put more seasoning in and . . .'

'It's all right,' she said. 'Now tell me. Where are you going on this holiday?'

He leaned back in his chair and smiled. 'Bali,' he said. 'Three weeks for the price of two. Leave your wallet behind. Food, drinks and watersports all free.'

'Lucky you,' she said and held up her glass. 'Let's drink to romance in the sun.'

He took a sip, then set his glass down on the table. 'What about you?'

'Nothing doing,' she said as lightly as she could manage. 'Matthew seems happily ensconced with wife – and daughter. I'm – on my own.' She stopped, took another sip of wine. 'Oh, I forgot. Wife now sending anonymous letters, just to add a touch of spice.'

Tom blinked. 'What? Surely you're not serious?'

'Yes, I am. To be honest,' she said, 'I only ever felt sorry for Jane. But Eloïse, Matthew's daughter. She's the manipulative one. She's clever. I still think after their holiday – I think Matthew would have left. But Eloïse is the sort of child who can act. So she fell into the part of a baby. Then her father couldn't leave.'

'No, he couldn't,' he said, nodding. 'Not Matthew.'

They were both silent for a moment, then Joanna gave a snort.

'Please, Tom,' she said, 'can we change the subject?'

He nodded. 'All right. How's your murder case going?'

'Slowly but surely,' she said, toying with her food.

'Do you have any idea who did her yet?'

She shook her head. 'Not really. But we're working on it.'

'The papers say the police were interviewing the ex-husband.'

She laughed at that. 'Did they?' She took another forkful of the peppered pork, chewed it and washed it down with a mouthful of wine. 'We've interviewed lots of people, including the ex-husband,' she admitted. 'But bear in mind something like sixty per cent of murders are done by the next of kin. Sam Finnigan seemed like a good place to start. Especially as he'd already been in front of the beak with a charge of ABH against his now-deceased wife.'

'Mmmm.' Tom was considering. 'And what about her most recent boyfriend?'

She sighed. 'The trouble with that is – who *was* Sharon Priest's most recent boyfriend? Paul Agnew says they split up when she was pregnant with Ryan. Somewhere along the line, somebody made her pregnant. We think it might have been a married lover – according to friends Sharon was having an affair with a married man.' She stopped and thought for a minute. 'The trouble is no one seems to know anything about him, except that he was married. Oh . . . I nearly forgot . . . married and *rich*.' She put her wine glass down.

'So where do your investigations take you next?'

'Macclesfield tomorrow, checking statements on Sunday, then on Monday we'll call in at Blyton's?'

'Blyton's?'

'She was a cleaner there. Mike and I are going to interview a few of her work mates. She'd put an ad in the lonely hearts column in the *Evening Standard*, and it's possible she might have talked about it at work.' She gave a snort. 'It was so corny, Tom – Prince Charming for a Cinderella in red. Honestly, I ask you.'

Tom frowned. 'And I thought women were so liberated these days – bringing up families on their own, divorcing, kicking out the boyfriends they'd got fed up with . . .'

'You may think that,' Joanna said, 'and for some this is true. But for many others what they really want is Prince Charming to come and sweep them off their feet.' She stopped. 'But he never does. All they get is a series of unsuitable boyfriends.' Tom shot her swift glance and she hurried on. 'Someone from this area answered that advert. But although she only put a box number the person who answered it used her name. He replied "Dear Sharon." And he knew other things about her, too.'

'Spooky.'

'The worrying thing's that we've found six or seven letters from the same source – from the man we believe she met at the pub the night she was murdered. They come from a . . .' Words almost failed her. 'He's a deviant,' she said, 'a nutcase. And he's almost certainly killed before. A girl from Macclesfield.'

'So that's why you're going to Macclesfield. I did wonder.'

She met his eyes. 'And there may be more.' A sudden burst of anger shot through her. 'How can Sharon have been so naive she didn't recognize him as a danger? Why did she arrange to meet him? Unless . . .'

'Unless what?'

A new idea was taking shape. 'Unless she suspected what he was and wanted to go.'

'Why on earth . . .?'

Her voice was low. 'Unless her perversions matched his.'

She drank deeply, then made a face. 'Then there are the usual loose ends guaranteed to drive any self-respecting detective wild. We still haven't found her other shoe. She was only wearing one when we found her body. We've scoured the moors. It just isn't there.' She stopped. 'We just wonder – it's a long shot, I know – but we just wonder whether it's still in the killer's car or somewhere near where she was killed. We live in hope,' she said. 'And as usual the wire cable she was killed with is proving annoyingly elusive to track down.'

She took another draught of wine. 'And it all matches this other rape and murder which took place in Macclesfield eighteen months ago.'

Tom looked interested. 'Really?'

She nodded. 'Another young single mother,' she said. 'Do you remember Stacey Farmer?'

Tom nodded.

'Same sort of set-up, really, advert in the local rag, wanting and promising the usual – sex and adventure. And she got it. Turned up raped and strangled on the edge of Macclesfield Forest. I'll speak to Matthew tomorrow to see if the DNA samples match, but I bet they do.'

Tom had a habit of saying least while he was thinking most, so although she knew he had listened to her every word he said nothing, but regarded her with intelligent eyes.

'The problem with DNA testing is,' she said. 'You can match like with like. But you can't screen the whole population. So we have to catch our sparrow first.' She stopped talking and set her knife and fork back on the plate. 'Well,' she said. 'That was quite – interesting.'

'Have I impressed you with my superb domesticity?' He glanced at the half-full plates. 'Oh well,' he said. 'Never mind.'

A nasty shock awaited her when Joanne approached her front door later that evening. There was a huge, bright red splatter over her front door. For one frozen moment she thought it was blood. Then she moved closer and smelt the paint. It was still wet. She stood and stared at it with one thought running through her mind.

'Jane.'

Chapter Ten

She awoke early and watched the sun, pale and cool, stream in through the bedroom window. She sat up, wrapped her arms around her knees and thought.

She couldn't mention Jane's spiteful attacks to Matthew. It would seem too much like telling tales from school. But she wanted her to stop and leave her alone. No more letters. No more tins of paint. No more Matthew.

So what *did* she really want? Marriage . . . children . . . home . . . She didn't care either way about marriage; children she had something approaching dislike for and she already had a home. She glanced around the bedroom with its discreet but pretty wallpaper and antique pine furniture. She was happy here.

So what was missing?

She stared out of the window at a blue tit pecking at the windowframe. Yes, what *was* she missing?

She had always thought, from early childhood, that study of the criminal mind, apprehension of felons . . . that it would all be enough. Her joy in detective novels had always been in the last chapter – the just desserts bit. But in the real world how many criminals did get their comeuppance? And how many innocent people were the ones to suffer? Perhaps that accounted for the lack of fulfilment she sometimes felt. It was true that her idealism had evaporated, but she had been warned that it would. She'd been told as a young rookie: 'Forget justice, Piercy. Being a copper is nothing to do with that. It's a matter of working the system.' But the compromises, the injustice of the entire adversarial system, made her unhappy. Break one of the countless rigid rules of PACE and the villains would go free. No matter who knew they were guilty.

Her pottery figures downstairs had all been apprehended within the law, sentenced by it.

A chill gripped her momentarily. Rob her of her faith in the work she did and what was left? Answer: very little.

What could she do about it?

She didn't know. She threw off the bedclothes. Perhaps something was missing from everybody's life.

It seemed natural to work the weeks through during a murder investigation. And as Joanna dressed again in a skirt and sweater on that Saturday morning she knew that even if she had taken the day off her mind would have stayed with the still figure on the moors. Like a Staffordshire bull terrier her grip would be maintained to the end.

But Korpanski was a family man and his wife resented the lonely weekends left with their children. She glowered at Joanna as she answered her knock.

'Mike,' she shouted back into the house.

Korpanski's face was flushed as he passed her. It

didn't take a clairvoyant to know they'd been rowing again.

Joanna waited in the car while Mike gave his wife a peck on the cheek. He climbed in and slammed the door. She was tempted to comment. They could be on the verge of a significant discovery.

He should have felt stimulated, excited – not guilty at abandoning his family. This was his job. Not for the first time she had no regrets about being single. Too many police marriages crashed against the rocks of long hours, unpredictable appearances, and sudden and prolonged disappearances.

The road to Macclesfield was quiet and the sun spilt across the fields to light the dew. It was such a contrast to last week's snow that it made Sharon's murder seem a long, long time ago.

As they followed the signs for the town centre she risked an approach to Mike. 'Spot of bother at home?' It was an attempt to lighten his mood, but it failed.

He grunted. 'She doesn't like me working weekends.'

There was no answer to that.

Detective Inspector Paul Austin was already in his office when they arrived. He had a brisk, pleasant attitude, an unremarkable face and steady brown eyes.

He briefly shook hands with them before settling behind his desk. 'I don't envy you,' he said. 'The Stacey Farmer case has haunted me for the last eighteen months. The sight of that poor girl . . .'

He stared out of the window for a moment. 'He

must have been a ruddy . . .' He drew in a deep breath. 'To tempt a girl out – on a date – and then do that to her. And I reckon he must have planned it, so I knew sooner or later he'd do the same thing again.' He ran his fingers through the short, brown hair. 'I've been waiting. But you know how it is. There's one sure way of getting more evidence.'

They all knew. A second murder provided fresh evidence yet there was no source they wanted less. Joanna felt a pang of sympathy for Paul Austin. 'You must have dreaded this moment.'

He nodded.

They spent more than an hour talking to him and at the end he pushed a red file towards them. 'I hope it gets you somewhere,' he said, 'although I have my doubts. Between you and me I don't think we even interviewed the right guy. I don't think we got any-where near him.'

He tapped the file. 'Maybe I'm wrong and there'll be something in there that can be used as evidence. I hope so. It would make me and the rest of the invest-igating officers feel a lot better.'

Joanna knew the feeling – the count of hours wasted when an investigation proved to be futile.

They drove back to Leek.

Weekends are an ideal time to find people at home so they had decided to spend the rest of Saturday and Sunday concentrating on the house-to-house inter-views. The estate was a large one, densely populated and people had plenty to say. The trouble was that most of it had little relevance to the investigation. By late Sunday night they had a pile of statements to be checked through as well as the file on the murder of Stacey Farmer. Joanna yawned and stretched her arms. 'I'd like to say I'll sit up all night reading these but I think it's more likely I'll fall asleep.' She eyed Mike across the desk. 'You'd better get home. Fran will wonder what's happened to you.'

Mike stood up. 'I think she has an idea,' he said shortly. 'I'll see you tomorrow.'

She couldn't be certain but she imagined Stuart had been waiting for her to turn out on to the main road. He grinned, gripped her hand in a hard handshake, rattled his feet into their pedals and together they cycled along the road. He seemed cock-a-hoop today and she was sure he would ask her out again. But he didn't.

She watched his muscled brown legs working the pedals. He was a good-looking man, with neat, regular features, athletic and fit looking.

So why wasn't she flattered that he chose to ride with her?

Mike was late at his desk and when he arrived he had the swollen face of a man who had eventually induced sleep with a heavy night's drinking. Around him clung the faint odour of last night's beer. He groaned as he walked in.

'I was praying you'd be late,' he said, 'that I'd have

time for a third cup of coffee and you wouldn't have cycled in. It makes you too bloody lively.'

She smiled sweetly, disappeared and returned with two cups of steaming coffee. She handed one to him and he sipped it cautiously.

'Thanks,' he said, wiping his sweating forehead. 'I need this.'

Joanna laughed.

Then he glanced at her crossed legs. 'You aren't working in those, are you?'

'No.' She looked down at the cycling shorts and nylon shirt and shook her head. 'Mike . . .' she paused. 'Can I ask your advice?' She felt suddenly unsure of herself.

He looked up.

'Someone threw a pot of red paint over my door two nights ago.'

'Someone?'

She was silent and he gave a low whistle. 'Matthew's wife, I suppose?'

She nodded. 'She's been writing me fan mail, too.'

Mike's dark eyes were thoughtful. 'If I were you, Jo,' he said, 'I'd leave it. Don't stir it up. She'll soon get bored.'

'But . . .'

He touched her arm. 'Leave it. Unless she does something worse.'

'OK. Thanks, Mike,' she said. 'Now, drink your coffee and we'll plan the day out. I want to go to Blyton's.'

He narrowed his eyes. 'What exactly are we looking for?'

'I don't know,' she said. 'I want to talk to that friend of hers. What was her name?'

'Andrea,' he said.

'She might be able to fill in some of the gaps. If only we could get the name of Ryan's father.' She paused for a moment, frowning. 'Why did Doreen Priest dislike him so much?'

'Hang on a minute,' Mike said. 'Who says she didn't like him? She said she didn't even know who he was.'

'She *said*.' Joanna stared at Mike. 'Come on, she must have known who he was. Otherwise why is she so against Ryan? He's only six months old. While she's quite prepared to have the other two she'll throw Ryan to the wolves. Why?'

Mike shrugged his shoulders and winced at the pain in his head.

'I suppose Andrea might know who it was that Finnigan found her in bed with,' she said slowly. 'And she just might be able to tell us something about Prince Charming, too. Someone at Blyton's must know more about Sharon Priest than we've discovered so far.'

Half an hour later, dressed more demurely in a navy suit, Joanna was driving Mike into the yard of the small, family-run engineering firm. She had decided to drive after taking the decision that Mike was possibly still over the legal limit. Certainly he was bleary eyed and looked tired. 'I ought to be breathalyzing you,' she said, 'instead of acting as your chauffeur.'

He smiled.

'You'd better take the rest of the day off,' she said, 'once we've been to Blyton's.'

She steered the car into the parking space, next to a familiar white Mercedes – number plate RED 36. She sat and stared at it.

'Well,' she said. 'An old friend.'

Mike screwed up his face in puzzlement.

'What a coincidence. Do you remember the night of the Legal Ball?' she said, still keeping her eyes fixed on the vehicle. 'The night you got me stopped and breathalyzed? The same night Sharon Priest was murdered?'

'Yes,' Mike said, giving her a sideways look. 'I remember.'

She climbed out of the car and stared at the white Merc.

'This car passed me.' She looked at Mike. 'It *tore* past me, coming straight from the moors. It was late, too, well after the snow had started. Do you remember I asked you about it? What did you say the owner's name was?'

She stood and recalled the black night, spattered with huge snowflakes, the car screaming past.

'Charles Haworth. He's an accountant.'

'And here he is, working at the same company as Sharon.'

Her eyes rested on Mike. 'Well,' she said, 'what do you think?'

Mike shrugged. 'I'll tell you what I don't think,' he said. 'I don't think it's a coincidence.'

She leaned forward. 'Then what *do* you think?'

'She'd been having an affair – hadn't she? With a

married man . . . someone Christine Rattle – and others – described as being wealthy.'

'She wasn't in the same class as this guy.'

'No?'

'She was a bloody cleaner.'

'She was a very attractive cleaner,' Joanna said. 'Attractive and available. And it looks as though he works here, at Blyton's. In the same place.'

Mike blinked. 'And he was on the moors that night?'

Again the picture swam into her vision, clear and unmistakable. She shook her head. 'Regretfully, no,' she said. 'It was throwing a blizzard down here, in the town. We decided Sharon's body was dumped before the snow started. It was late when I saw him. Wherever he'd been it wasn't the moors. Oh well, nice try. But still, he did come from the direction of the Buxton road, which must have been closed for at least an hour before I saw him. He might have seen something.'

They climbed out of the car and entered the factory, which was dirty and noisy and stank of soldering flux, hot metal and grease. They picked their way past the machinery and through the noise until they reached a door marked 'office', which sealed in thick carpets and the scent of lavender. A young woman with brown hair, teased into an improbable ponytail, stood up as they entered. She rubbed her hands down the side of her skirt. 'Can I help you?' she asked.

Joanna nodded. 'I'm Detective Inspector Piercy. I'd like to speak to whoever's in charge, please.'

'Can you wait a minute?' the girl lisped. 'He's got someone with him at the moment.'

'Would that be a Mr Haworth?' Mike asked brusquely.

The girl blinked. 'We're not supposed to divulge . . .'

'It's all right,' Joanna said resignedly. 'We want to speak to him too.'

They sat down and waited.

The girl glanced across periodically. 'He's our accountant,' she said eventually.

When the door finally opened, a distinguished, grey-haired man walked out. He was wearing a navy business suit somewhat spoiled by a bright yellow silk tie which gave him a foppish, effeminate air.

Joanna stood up. 'Mr Haworth?'

He turned a pair of alert grey eyes on her. 'Yes?'

'I'm Detective Inspector Piercy,' Joanna said.

He held out a large hand and gave hers a firm shake. 'Hello,' he said with a wide, warm smile. And quite unexpectedly Joanna found herself liking the man.

'We're investigating the murder of Sharon Priest,' she said. 'Did you know her?'

Haworth looked vaguely puzzled. 'Sorry?' he queried.

'She was a cleaner here.'

'Actually,' he said, 'I'm the accountant.' A ripple of humour passed across his face. 'I don't really have a great deal to do with the cleaners.'

Behind Mike the girl with the unruly ponytail spluttered.

'I know that.' Joanna was forced to put a little steel into her voice. 'But I really would like to talk to you. Would tomorrow suit? Shall we say about eleven? At your offices?'

Haworth looked amazed. 'What on earth do you want to ask me?'

'We're interviewing everyone who knew her.'

'But I've told you,' he said. 'I *didn't* know her.' He paused for a moment, frowning. 'Couldn't you ask me any questions here? Do you have to visit my offices?'

'Well, yes, we do, Mr Haworth,' Joanna said. 'You see, I've come here to talk to the MD and other employees of Blyton's today.' She stopped. 'I want to visit you separately.'

He still looked puzzled but nodded briefly, his eyes wary. Then again he showed a faint touch of humour. 'I don't suppose, Detective Inspector Piercy, that I have any choice in the matter, do I?'

And now she was smiling too. 'No, Mr Haworth,' she said, 'you don't.'

'I thought not. Well, my offices are in Bath Street, near the top. But I assure you I know nothing about this . . . You said she was a cleaner?'

Joanna nodded.

'Until tomorrow, then,' he said, before turning on his heel and walking through the swing doors, leaving behind him a faint tang of expensive aftershave.

'What a wanker,' Mike said under his breath.

Joanna turned to him. 'I thought he was rather nice.'

Mike gave an explosive grunt.

The girl with the ponytail was speaking into the phone.

Joanna turned to see a short, balding man come out of the office and stand in the doorway. 'Detective Inspector Piercy?' he asked.

She nodded and introduced Mike.

'Richard Barratt,' he said. 'Managing Director.' He glanced from one to the other. 'Dreadful business,' he said. 'Dreadful business.' But his eyes were cold and wary. 'Naturally, only too anxious to help. You'd like some coffee?'

'Thank you.'

'Sarah . . .' He glanced at the girl with a ponytail. 'Do the honours, will you, dear?'

Joanna and Mike followed Richard Barratt into a spacious office lined with blue carpet and mahogany and he motioned them to chairs and then sat behind his desk. 'Now, what exactly can I do for you?'

'Tell me about Sharon Priest,' Joanna began.

The MD sighed. 'Very sad. Tragic, in fact.' He lowered his voice. 'Do you know yet when the funeral will be? We want to send flowers. You know . . .' he finished inadequately.

'What sort of a person was she?' Joanna asked. 'How long had she worked here?'

'Nearly three years,' Richard Barratt said. 'She was . . . quite a good worker.' He gave an apologetic smile. 'You understand. There were the odd dirty corners. I expect she spent a bit too much time leaning on her brush . . . But she did turn up. And when I had words with her she was always quite helpful – and polite,' he added.

'Did you know anything of her personal life?'

'No. No.' This time his voice was emphatic. 'Nothing. I knew she had children. Split up with her husband. According to her records she had a couple of

169

months' maternity leave for the two youngest. Apart from that, nothing.'

'Did she have many friends here?'

'I think she was quite pally with the other cleaner. They worked together, of course, although I sometimes thought it was a little counter-productive.' His face grew hard. 'I'm sure I would have got much more than half the work done with just one cleaner.' He stopped, gave a false smile. 'But this is a large factory. They were reluctant to come alone. But chatting time plus cup of tea time. Well . . .' He waved his hands around. The coffee arrived and the next few minutes were spent watching Sarah prettily sorting out milk and sugar, stirring and passing the cups around. Joanna returned to the subject of the other cleaner.

'You can speak to her here,' Richard Barratt said. 'She works in the canteen at lunchtimes, then comes back for the evenings.'

'Are any of the other employees still here in the evenings?'

Richard Barratt thought for a moment. 'Well, I suppose some of the reps – if they're late back. The engineers, if they're in the middle of something.' He stopped. 'There's no law against them working a little over their normal hours.' Again they were treated to a wolfish smile.

'What hours did Sharon Priest work?'

'Five till seven thirty, Monday to Friday. The work force finish at five, you see?'

They both nodded.

'And where were you last Tuesday night?'

'Here, I'm afraid,' Barratt said ruefully. 'There's an

awful lot of paperwork these days, especially with VAT and the export business so competitive.' He glanced quickly from one to the other. 'It's the only way I can survive in business, by working virtually all the hours God sends.'

Mike spoke. 'You often work late, Mr Barratt?'

'Oh, yes,' he said innocently.

'While the cleaners are here?'

At this Barratt picked up the message and began to splutter. 'If you're implying . . .' he said.

'We're not implying anything, Mr Barratt,' Joanna said sharply. 'We're trying to find out who raped then murdered one of your employees.'

Barratt went pale. 'Quite, quite.' He swallowed. 'What I was trying to say was that I always worked here, in my office. The cleaners only came in if the office was empty.' He recovered enough to give another of his unpleasant smiles.

'At what time did you leave last Tuesday?'

Barratt frowned, rubbed the centre of his forehead. 'Eleven,' he said, 'eleven thirty. I'm not too sure.'

'You're married, Mr Barratt?'

'Yes,' he said resignedly. 'Long-suffering wife.' He gave a hollow laugh and Joanna and Mike glanced at one another.

Joanna decided to tackle the subject head on. 'Rumour has it Sharon was having an affair with a married man, Mr Barratt,' she said. 'I don't suppose you have any ideas?'

He looked blank. 'I'm sorry, I miss out on all the factory-floor gossip. I never hear any of it.' He smiled apologetically. 'Being the MD, they all shut up like clams the minute I walk in.'

'So you know nothing more?' Mike sounded sceptical.

Barratt was still unembarrassed. 'I'm sorry,' he said again. 'I don't.'

'OK.' Joanna smiled. 'Thanks.'

She glanced at Mike and he spoke casually. 'What do you make here at Blyton's?'

For the first time during the interview Barratt looked at ease. 'We're a small engineering company,' he said. 'We make anything to order.'

'Is that so?' Mike produced the cable. 'You don't make stuff like this?'

Barratt picked it up, gave it a full and considered study before handing it back, shaking his head. 'No', he said. 'Nothing like this. Sorry.'

There was no trace of recognition in his voice.

Joanna stood up. 'Would you mind if we interviewed the other employees?' she asked.

'Not at all,' he said genially. 'Use my office. I can work out there with Sarah.'

There were more than thirty employees at Blyton's and from twenty-seven of them they learned nothing.

The reps were out on the road and two full-time engineers here at a conference for the day.

It wasn't until Andrea Farr bounced in that the visit to Blyton's became worthwhile.

She was a pretty, lively chestnut-haired girl with liquid dark eyes. She smiled at Joanna sadly.

'I still can't believe it about Sharon,' she said, her eyes threatening to fill with tears. 'I can't believe someone would kill her. Why?' She looked beseechingly at Joanna. 'Why did they?' She hesitated for a moment, glanced knowingly at Mike. 'Sex?'

Joanna nodded. 'It looks like it.'

Andrea Farr sat down heavily. 'Do you think it was the bloke from the advert?'

'We think so,' Joanna said quietly.

'I helped her write that,' she said in a small, shocked voice. 'Me and her. We did it together. And then she showed her friend Christine . . .'

'Andrea,' she said softly, 'tell me about the advert.'

'She had absolutely loads of replies,' she said fiercely. 'Loads.' Then she looked at Mike with puzzlement in her face. 'Why did she have to choose that one?'

Andrea blinked back tears. 'She was so bored, she said. Bored and fed up. I think that's why—.' She pulled herself up.

'Why what?'

'She did all sorts of things.'

'You mean the advert?'

'Not just that.' Andrea looked troubled. 'There was Ryan too.'

'Ryan?'

'Well, she was hard up. She needed money. It was a good way to make money. Lots of it.'

It was Joanna who had to put it into words. 'Do you mean that she gave birth to Ryan for this man?'

'Well, he wasn't never going to marry her, was he?' Andrea's answer was unexpectedly fierce. 'Men like that don't marry women like us. They use us.' More of the fighter spilled out then. 'But she was going to get plenty of money out of him.'

Then Joanna understood.

Andrea continued. 'The trouble came after Ryan was born. She couldn't bear to give him up, you see. That's what she fell out with her mum about. Her mum knew she could have done with the money. But Sharon was on to a winner because he gave her the money and she still got to keep Ryan.' She smiled and wiped the corner of her mouth. 'She just strung him along. So he never got anything out of her at all.'

'I expect he was angry about that,' Mike prompted, but Andrea merely shrugged. 'Dunno,' she said. 'Sharon never told me.'

Joanna drew in a deep sigh. This whole case was full of Sharon's friends who all sang the same chorus. *Sharon never told me.*

'So who was this bloke?' Mike asked casually.

The question again provoked the same blank look, the same chorus.

'Dunno.'

'Oh, come on . . .' Mike sounded angry. But Andrea faced him bravely. 'I don't know,' she said. 'I really don't. It's no use your bullying me. I can't tell what I don't know.'

'But he worked here.' Mike's voice was tense.

'I thought he did. I wasn't absolutely sure.' She frowned. 'Sharon never said. She just let me think he worked here. I might have been barking up the wrong tree.'

'You must have had some idea who he was.'

'You wouldn't understand,' she said, smiling. 'That was half the fun, not knowing. I'd look at everyone and wonder. Was it him? Was it him?'

'But there aren't that many people working here,' Joanna objected.

'There's enough,' Andrea said grimly. 'There's Barratt. Mr Barratt,' she said. 'Sometimes I'd look at him and wonder. But,' she giggled nervously, 'I couldn't imagine the two of them together. And there's two supervisors and the engineers.'

She suddenly looked shrewd. 'Doesn't Christine know who he was?'

Joanna shook her head.

'Or Sharon's mum?'

Andrea looked at them both. 'Sharon was a very loyal person.' She was good to him. She kept his secret. Because if I don't know, nor Christine, nor her mum, then no one knows.' She stopped. 'Except him.'

Joanna decided to move the subject on. 'Tell me about the advert,' she said. 'About the one date she decided to go on. Why him?'

Andrea thought for a moment before speaking. 'Well, she said there was something about his letters.' She paused, then looked at Joanna. 'She seemed drawn, like a moth to a flame. That was how she put it. She was sort of – fascinated by him. Said he was clever. And besides, she was a bit curious really. I mean, he knew her name, and she hadn't put it in the ad.'

'Are you sure she hadn't?'

Andrea looked slightly irritated. 'Yes,' she said. 'She didn't give her name. So how could he have known?

She always used the box number. He wrote back "Dear Sharon".'

'She must have known she was taking a risk,' Mike said curiously.

Andrea turned to him. 'Well,' she said. 'Sharon thought she could turn up at the pub . . . you know . . . in her new dress, looking nice. And when he came, if she felt safe, she could stay. But if she didn't she could drive herself straight home.' She gave Mike a flirtatious glance and Joanna smirked as Mike flushed right to the roots of his black hair. 'She was dying to know who he was.' She looked animated and both Mike and Joanna had a sudden, vivid picture of Sharon with this girl, giggling and puzzling over the answer to her call for a Prince Charming. 'It was a real mystery. Wild horses wouldn't have kept her away from the Quiet Woman that night. We'd spent ages deciding what to put in that advert,' she said. 'Laughed like anything we did.'

Mike leaned closer. 'Could anyone have heard you talking about it?' he asked.

'I suppose so,' she said. 'We weren't really hiding anything.'

She rang Matthew from her office. He sounded unaccountably relieved to hear her voice.

'Joanna,' he said. 'I've been trying to get hold of you.'

She wished she didn't feel so glad.

'I want to talk to you, Joanna – please. *Please.*' His voice had never sounded so desperate.

'Oh, Matthew,' she said, exasperated. 'What is the point?'

'That's what I want to talk to you about.'

'Can't you speak over the phone?'

'Not for what I want to say. I must see you, Joanna.'

She steeled herself to say nothing about the pot of paint.

'Look, Matthew, you *know* I'm busy at the moment.'

'But you don't understand.'

'Oh, I do,' she said, 'only too well. Now please tell me the results of the tests.'

He paused for a moment then said, 'Your instincts were correct. The Macclesfield case matches your victim's.'

'You're sure?'

'Absolutely. There's no doubt about it.'

'So it's the same guy?'

'Yes. He's a double-rapist and killer.' He paused and when he spoke again she knew he was smiling. 'I'm not trying to tell you your job, Jo, but if I were you I'd be looking at other rape cases in the area.'

'Really?' She allowed herself a tight smile. 'I've been doing just that for the last two days.'

'I might have known.' He laughed.

'Thank you, Matthew.'

'Anything else I can do for you?'

She smiled. 'Not at the moment. How's Eloïse?' She didn't even know why she had asked it.

Matthew cleared his throat. 'Going through a phase of trying to starve me back home.'

'What?'

'That's what I've been trying to tell you, Jo,' he said patiently. 'I've left Jane. I've moved out.'

The room swam.

'When?'

'A week ago.' He paused. 'I didn't want to tell you – not straight away. I had a lot of thinking to do. And I knew there would be problems with Jane and Eloïse . . . And there have been,' he added reluctantly.

'I see.'

'Look. I'm away from tomorrow on a forensic conference in Blackpool. Can I see you when I get back?'

'Yes,' she said in a voice so quiet even she could hardly hear it.

Then the line went dead.

WPC Cheryl Smith popped her head round the door. 'Colclough wants to see you,' she said. 'And he looks like thunder.'

Arthur Colclough was standing staring out of the window when she walked in.

'This is a small town, Piercy,' he said slowly. 'People know their police force.'

'Yes, sir.' And with a sinking heart she thought she knew where the conversation was going to go.

He turned round then, sat behind his desk and motioned her to the chair opposite.

'How are your investigations getting on, Piercy?'

'Steadily, sir.'

'Anywhere near making an arrest?'

She shook her head. 'Not really, sir. But I've had

word from the lab. The Macclesfield case and our one were done by the same man. The DNA samples match.'

'Mmm.' He looked up and she saw his eyes were tired.

She waited.

'Ahem.' He cleared his throat noisily and returned to his original topic. 'This is a small town, Piercy. And it doesn't like scandal, especially amongst its police force.' He looked embarrassed. 'I have to tell you that certain allegations have been made against you.' He cleared his throat again. 'Immorality. Adultery.' His eyes bored straight into hers. 'Ugly words, but not half as ugly as the poison I'm getting in unsigned letters nearly every morning in my postbag. Piercy, someone doesn't like you.'

'Sir . . .?'

Colcough met her eyes. 'You know – more than anyone – just how much the force demands of its coppers, especially at Detective Inspector level. Be careful.' His bulldog chin wobbled. 'Scandal could destroy your chances in the force.'

'But, sir . . .'

He glared at her. 'What a man might get away with on that score would be enough to slide you back down the ranks again, Piercy. You're a woman. You may not like it, but women are judged *very differently*.'

Chapter Eleven

It had been waiting to happen.

The gratification he had derived from the shoe had made him a slave to its pleasures. Sometimes he didn't wait for Lizzie to go out, but waited until she was planted in front of her favourite TV programme. Then he would slip into the garage, fumble on top of the tin cupboard until he found the box.

Then he would fondle the shoe and dream . . .

Lizzie opened the door ever so gently, tiptoed in the dark, passing the car.

She took two steps forward and stopped, her face a picture of revulsion. 'Oh . . !' she said. 'Oh . . !'

There was no point even trying to keep it behind his back.

'Whose is it?' she whispered, and he knew she wouldn't believe he had never met its owner. He stared at her helplessly.

She walked around it, staring – not at him, but at it – studying it with a grim face.

'I see,' she said. 'Meeting tarts again, are we?'

Her lips pressed hard together. 'I told you, Andrew,' she said with soft venom. 'I did warn you, didn't I?'

'Please, Lizzie.'

Her eyes were hard. 'I'm listening,' she said, 'to whatever story you're cooking up today. I'm listening, but whatever you say I'm not going to believe you.'

But Andrew Donovan's desperate mind was starting to work. And, much as he feared Lizzie, they *were* married. Two girls, late teens, left home. He didn't really want a divorce. He was comfortable here. And in a way he accepted his frumpy wife, flat heels and all. He was used to her. Most of his amorous trips came to fruition only in his mind. But his realistic side told him there was only one way to make Lizzie believe the story he was about to tell her.

She had become accustomed to Stuart's appearance on her morning cycle route. Cycling was more pleasant in pairs and she had noticed she was moving faster now, challenged by his speed. He was good company, but he had renewed his invitation and when she had refused he had appeared to take it as a challenge.

And her future with Matthew?

She pedalled faster, a joyful song in her heart. The event she had thought would never happen. He had left Jane.

'You seem happy today.'

She glanced across at him, smiling. 'I've had some good news?'

'What sort of good news?' He gave her a strange look.

And she found she didn't want to tell him. Because she suddenly felt uneasy about his reaction.

'Oh, just something to do with a friend,' she said vaguely.

'What?' He was pedalling slower now, holding her up. It was making her wobble slightly.

'A friend of mine,' she said squarely. 'Some good news.' She pedalled faster, but he caught up with her, clamped his fist on her handlebars.

'What?'

'It's private,' she said crossly.

He let go with a suddenness that almost toppled her from her bike and she was left with an uncomfortable impression of a vicious, furious face.

She was glad when she reached the turn-off and bumped into Mike in the car park.

He nodded towards the lithe figure, bent over his handlebars, disappearing up the road.

'Still got your travelling companion, I see.'

She gave a short outburst of breath. 'Unfortunately,' she said.

'And I thought you two were the best of friends.'

'He's a very strange person.' Then she grinned at Mike. 'Your turn to get the coffee today,' she said.

He was back a moment later with two steaming polystyrene cups. 'So what's on the agenda today?'

'I want to go over the statements from everyone at the Quiet Woman that night,' she said. 'Especially the barmaids'. Then we've got an appointment with Mr Charles Haworth, accountant. And,' she added, 'who knows what else?'

Mike nodded and handed her a complaints slip. 'By the way,' he said. 'I thought you'd like to know, your cleaner had a brick thrown through her window last night.'

'Christine?'

He nodded. 'I don't know whether it has anything to do with the case, but . . . Anyway, I thought you'd want to know.'

'Was there a note thrown too, or just a brick?'

Mike glanced down at the slip.

> *Don't interfear in things what don't concern you.*
> *Stop rattling else it'll be your legs next.*

He glanced at her. 'Recognize the terminology?'

'Twenty guesses. And they all spell Finnigan,' she said grimly. 'Get hold of the original note and send it to forensics. If he's trying to silence a witness . . .' She looked at Mike. 'By God, I'll have him.'

Mike took a long sip of coffee. 'What I want to know is,' he said, his eyes meeting hers thoughtfully, 'what's Finnigan got to hide?'

She made a quick decision. 'We'll call in at Christine's on the way to Haworth's,' she said. 'He can wait a minute.' A sudden anger streaked through her. 'Let him stew,' she said.

They settled down to comb through the statements.

'What exactly are we looking for?' Mike asked.

'I just wondered,' she replied slowly, leafing through the sheaf of papers. 'Did anybody notice whether Sharon seemed to recognize the man?'

It was hard to find. People had noticed so little that evening. All had been immersed in their own conversations or wondering about the weather. Did they dare stay for one more drink and risk being caught by the threatened snow? In fact only Dianne, a young woman who had fallen out with her boyfriend that night, had been sitting opposite Sharon Priest and had noted the expression on her face.

'She looked as though it had been a good joke,' she had said. And Sharon had stood up and said hello . . . and 'Oh, it's you.' And later on in the statement Dianne said she'd looked disappointed.

'So she did know him. And what's more, it wasn't who she'd hoped it would be.'

Mike stood up. 'So the ninety million dollar questions are,' he said: 'Who did she hope it would be? And who was it?'

She looked at him thoughtfully. 'I think we're getting nearer,' she said.

Christine's house was easy to spot from the end of the road. Four or five people were clustered at the garden wall, staring. They moved back, muttering, as the police car drew up outside and Joanna and Mike climbed out.

Christine's neat front garden shone with slivers of glass. The window itself was shattered with a jagged hole. They pushed open the gate and walked the few steps to the front door.

Christine was sitting in the lounge, a cigarette in her hand, watching the smoke waft delicately through the broken pane. She didn't even look up as they walked in.

'Bloody starers,' she said. 'Look at them – gawping. Love misfortune.' Her cigarette was dangling from trembling fingers. 'I heard it, you know. Late. In the middle of the night.'

Joanna noticed how pale her face was.

'It made such a bloody noise,' she said. 'I heard someone running. I was lying there, in bed, too frightened to come down and see what was going on.' She swallowed. 'I lay still until dawn. I thought he might come back. Then I rang the police.'

'Finnigan?' Mike spoke angrily.

Christine Rattle looked at him with weary eyes. 'What does it matter who it was?' she said. 'You can't do anything.' She set a match to another cigarette. 'No one will've seen him. And even if anyone did they won't say, else they'll get a little brick packet too.'

It was the cold cynicism that shocked Joanna.

'And even if you get a conviction,' Christine carried on, 'he won't get a custodial. He'll get a fine.' Her eyes narrowed. 'And how the fuck is he going to pay a fine? He's on the bloody dole.' She looked at Joanna angrily. 'So there you are, Detective Inspector of the Toyland Police Force. There you are. I gets a brick through my window. And he gets sod all.'

Her eyes dropped. 'What if I'd been watching telly,' she asked, 'with the kids? What if they'd been blinded?' Her eyes were moist and she put a hand up to cover her face. 'This is my home,' she said. 'It isn't worth a lot. But it's all I've got – me and my kids. Someone just invaded it.'

'Where are the children?'

'At my mum's. I got them there first thing. I don't feel safe here.'

'Christine.' Joanna sat down on the sofa. 'Why did he do it?'

And now she saw real fear in the woman's eyes. Christine licked her lips.

'Come on, Christine.' Mike was standing over her. 'Even Finnigan wouldn't shoot a brick through your window for nothing.' He was exasperated. 'For goodness' sake.'

Christine seemed to shrink into the settee. Joanna shot Mike a swift glance. The girl was terrified and the thought wormed its way into her mind. Finnigan was by all accounts a violent man. What if he had preferred violent sex? But looking at Christine's hand shake as she put her cigarette to her lips, Joanna hesitated to ask the question. And it seemed that it would not have been answered anyway.

The cigarette was dragged on three times in rapid succession and ground out before Christine spoke again. 'Leave me alone,' she pleaded. 'Please, just leave me alone.'

It was the last thing Joanna wanted to do. All her instincts were to winkle the truth out of Christine before offering her protection, but she was stuck, limited by police rules, so she took the only option open to her. 'We can protect you.'

Christine looked up with a world-weary face. 'For how long?' she demanded. 'The rest of my life? They get out, you know, settle old scores.'

She was silent for a minute before moving to more practical matters. 'Who's going to put new glass in?' she said. 'The council take ages and I can't afford it.'

The room was draughty and cold, wind whistling

through the splintered glass. Christine threw a glance at the shards still lying around the guilty brick in the centre of the carpet.

'The police took the paper,' she said. 'I expect you've seen it.'

'When I get back to the station.'

Christine nodded. 'I've rung the council.' Her voice was tired. 'They said they'd come round later.' She rubbed her eyes with her hands. 'I can't cope with this,' she said. 'I can't.'

She looked mournfully at Joanna. 'And I don't know when I'll next be able to come to work,' she said, running her fingers through her hair. 'I haven't felt right ever since Sharon died. Things aren't the same any more.' She puffed away at her cigarette. 'They just don't seem normal.'

There was no answer to that.

'The damn of it is,' Joanna said to Mike as they closed the garden gate behind them, 'we can't eliminate anyone from our enquiries . . . and definitely not Sam Finnigan.'

'Maybe we should call on him again,' Mike said. 'I'd like to have a word with him.'

'Careful, Mike,' she warned. 'Finnigan is just the type to retaliate at a vulnerable woman with a few kids to bring up on her own. He's a bully-boy.' She stopped and looked at him. 'But you're right. This does bring him even further under suspicion. We'll bring him in. To the station this time.'

Mike's eyes were dark when he stared at her. As

they climbed back into the squad car Joanna was glad to see council workmen draw up outside with a sheet of replacement glass.

'Should we put her under police protection?'

Joanna shook her head slowly. 'We'll just alert local bobbies . . . the ones on the beat.' She glanced at him. 'The one I want watched is Finnigan.' She watched the cluster of people grow smaller in the rear-view mirror and hoped this was not to prove a terrible mistake.

Haworth's office was in a pretty, traditional building standing at the top of Bath Street, pale green fancy blinds in Dickensian bowed windows. It looked prosperous, secure. They pulled up outside.

The obligatory receptionist sat at a desk. She wore a calf-length split skirt which revealed her long, skinny thighs until she stood up, when it drew modestly like curtains. She eyed both Joanna and Mike before speaking, then uttered just one word. 'Police?'

Joanna nodded.

'He was expecting you half an hour ago,' the girl said severely before adding, 'He's a very busy man.'

'Something cropped up, love,' Mike said, leaning over her. 'So just give him a call, will you?'

The girl was impervious to Mike's charm. She gave him a haughty look and disappeared through the door marked 'Charles Haworth'.

She came back a minute later and sat down carefully before she spoke. 'Mr Haworth will see you in a minute.' And she resumed some typing.

Sure enough, a minute later the door opened and

Haworth was standing in front of them, unsmiling. Less charming this time.

'I don't have a lot of time,' he said. 'I have an appointment.'

'I'm sorry,' Joanna explained. 'We had a problem. A brick thrown through someone's window.'

'Oh dear,' Haworth said. 'Well, do come in.'

Joanna gave Mike a quick glance and frowned. Something had altered Haworth. It was difficult to say what. She simply had the feeling that someone had touched a raw nerve.

Haworth led the way into his office. It too was traditional, furnished with antiques and clever drapes. An oil painting of a racehorse hung on the wall behind him. Its body glistening with the sheen of a fine race. The painting looked valuable.

Charles Haworth leaned back in his fine mahogany chair and pressed his fingertips together. 'All right,' he said. 'Fire away.'

Joanna knew he was trying to intimidate her. She met his grey eyes. 'You are the only accountant who works for Blyton's?'

Haworth's eyes narrowed. 'What on earth has all this got to do with . . .?'

'I'll ask the questions, Mr Haworth.' Joanna's voice was commanding. 'Are you?'

Haworth leaned forward. 'Detective Inspector,' he said slowly. 'Blyton's is a small, family-run firm employing about thirty people. One accountant is plenty.'

She nodded with a faint smile.

'I've been with him ever since I first went into

practice,' Haworth continued. 'Richard Barratt and I were at the same boarding school.' A trace of humour crossed his face. 'We shared the same dorm, Detective Inspector. He was the one who hauled me out of the toilet after my first "flushing". Friends like that are made for life.'

'I'm sure.' Joanna risked a swift glance at Mike. He was purple. 'Do you spend much time at Blyton's?'

'I'm there a couple of times a month.'

She nodded. 'Days?' she asked casually.

'Sometimes.' Haworth was being careful. 'Occasionally Richard and I work in the evenings. We are friends,' he said again.

'As you've said, Mr Haworth. Did you meet Sharon Priest there?'

Haworth sighed. 'I don't even know what she looked like.'

Mike fingered the snapshot of Sharon Priest, one of the many they had removed from her house. He flicked it on to the desk. 'Have a look at that,' he said.

Slowly Haworth leant over and looked at the photograph. He licked his lips. 'I might – I might have seen her,' he said.

'Take a better look,' Mike said brusquely. 'She was a good-looking girl. Worth a second glance.'

Haworth picked up the photograph then and stared at it. 'Yes,' he said carefully.

'Yes what?'

'I did see her there, I think, once or twice.'

'Did you ever speak to her?'

Haworth looked from one to the other. 'I don't know,' he said. 'I can't remember. I might have.'

'Which was it?' Mike asked doggedly. 'You don't know, you might have done, or you can't remember?'

'I think she made us tea once,' Haworth growled.

'I see.'

Joanna paused. 'Are you married Mr Haworth?'

He looked up. 'Yes,' he said. 'I am. Happily.'

'You have children?'

Haworth stared. 'No, but what the hell has this got to do with that poor woman's murder?' he demanded.

Joanna stared at him. 'I don't know – yet – Mr Haworth,' she said. 'Sharon had three children.'

Haworth looked at her. 'What's happened to them?' he asked.

'They've been taken into care. Their father is unfit to look after them.'

Haworth stared. His mouth was working for a few seconds before he finally spoke. 'Then what?' he asked.

'Their grandmother has agreed to care for October and William,' she said. 'However the baby . . .'

His face was locked on to hers.

'The baby may well be put up for adoption,' she said 'in the event of there being no blood relative deemed suitable.'

Haworth licked his lips again. 'I see,' he said quietly, and something of the urbane manner filtered back.

'Mr Haworth,' Joanna said, 'I have to ask you. Where were you on Tuesday night?'

'I was at home,' he lied comfortably. 'In with my wife – all night. I'm rather glad I didn't go out,' he said conversationally. 'It was snowing, wasn't it? Rather hard.'

Joanna nodded. 'Yes. It was – snowing rather hard. The snow in fact concealed Sharon's body for two days. She lay there out in the snow, frozen, dead.'

Haworth winced. 'Do you mind?' he said. 'Is this really necessary? Aren't you being rather theatrical – and tasteless?'

'I think murder is both those things,' Joanna said quietly. She stood up. 'Thank you very much for your help, Mr Haworth.'

He looked wary. 'I can't really see how I've been a help.'

'No?' Joanna gave a frank, disarming smile. 'Of course, I'll want to speak to you again,' she said as she and Mike filed out of the room.

'He lied,' she said when she was back in the car. 'He bloody lied. He *was* out that night. I saw him.'

'But no snow on the car?'

'He was still out,' Joanna insisted. 'He passed me. I don't get muddled over numberplates, Korpanski.'

Mike grinned at her. 'Want a sandwich?' he said and she nodded.

They ate them back at the station, washed down with Diet Coke.

'So what next?' Joanna said.

Mike was ramming the last of his sandwich into his mouth. Eating fast became a bad habit picked up during murder investigations. One never knew how long one would be allowed to eat, or when the next meal might be, and they were usually snatched sand-

wiches washed down with Coke. Joanna yearned for a
decent meal, and time to enjoy it.

Mike spoke with his mouth full. 'I wondered if we
should go round and see Deborah Pelham's family,' he
said. 'I know we spoke to them before, but there might
be something.'

'Korpanski,' she said. 'It has to be better than sitting
here reading these statements.'

Right on cue the telephone rang and Mike picked
it up. 'OK . . . I'll come and have a look.'

Joanna was only half listening. The name of
Deborah Pelham had stimulated her. Her mind was
busy as Mike left the room. And now the name began
to reach her, wires crossing and uncrossing before
finally she made the connection.

The name had been vaguely familiar all the way
through, running like a silver thread.

Leanne Ferry.

Now living with Paul Agnew, Sharon Priest's ex
live-in lover.

She sat still for a long while. And that was how
Mike found her when he walked in and put something
down on her desk. 'Take a look at this,' he said tri-
umphantly.

Chapter Twelve

She stared at the shoe almost superstitiously before touching it. Then she looked up at Mike. 'You're sure it's the one?'

He nodded.

'Where did it come from?'

He sat down with a puzzled look. 'It was brought in by a man called Andrew Donovan. He says he's a stocking salesman. His story is that he found it on the moors on the Wednesday morning after Sharon was killed. And guess what?' Mike grinned. 'He wants to make a statement.'

She looked at him shrewdly. 'Why now, Mike, a whole week later?'

'That's what I wondered.'

'He's outside?'

'Biting his fingernails. Accompanied by a dragon of a wife.'

She glanced at the shoe. 'Doesn't exactly look new any more, does it?' She studied the stains. 'We'd better send this for forensics,' she said, then, 'What's he been up to?'

Mike grinned. 'Come on, Joanna,' he said. 'Don't be naive. He's been a dirty old man with it.'

She flushed. 'OK,' she said. 'Bring him in in a minute. I want to have a word with you first.' And she related her thoughts to him.

'And this Leanne's living with Agnew?' he asked.

Joanna nodded.

Mike's eyebrows shot up. 'What a beggar of a little case, Jo,' he said.

'I'll call round to Pelham's home this evening,' she said. 'Just ask him a few questions . . . see if anything was left out of his original statements.' She met his eyes. 'But I admit I'm worried. We know about two – Sharon and Stacey. What if there are more that we just don't know about?'

She sat back in her chair. 'Do you know how many missing women there have been in this area in the last three years?'

Mike shrugged. 'Sixty?' he guessed.

'One hundred and eighty,' she said. 'About sixty a year – young women who have disappeared and never turned up again.'

She paused. 'Now you know, Mike, most of these leave after family arguments and they've simply filtered through to big cities . . . London, Manchester . . . some of them abroad. Most of the women I'm sure are still alive. But they're a vulnerable group. Vulnerable and mobile, hard to trace. And if anything had happened to even three a year, who would know? We wouldn't, and neither would their families. So we don't know what we've got on our hands. A man who's killed twice – or more? And if more, how many more?'

He shifted uneasily and she spoke again. 'Exactly.

So we'd better get our fingers out and find who's responsible.'

She jerked her thumb towards the door. 'What about him, Mike?'

He made a face, shook his head. 'Fits in some ways,' he said. 'A bit pathetic – dominated. But no, I don't think so, somehow.'

'Why not?' She looked curiously at him.

He took a deep breath. 'I can't see Sharon Priest even being tempted by a guy like that. She wouldn't have gone off with him. She would have gone home.'

Joanna nodded. She moved to the window and stared out. Perhaps it had been bad planning to extend the police station in such a way that her own office window looked on to nothing but a painted brick wall. It was a little too symbolic. But they weren't meeting a brick wall in this case. It was more a case of catacombs, long dark tunnels . . . too many of them. And only one would eventually lead to the man who had met Sharon that night at the Quiet Woman.

She gave a heartfelt sigh before turning back to Mike. 'We'll use the large interview room,' she said. 'Did you say his wife is with him?'

'Yes.'

'Does he want a solicitor?'

'He says not. His wife is the only person he wants to witness what he has to say.'

She nodded and together she and Mike walked along the corridor to the interview room.

She looked curiously at the short, balding man with a meek air, dressed in a cheap grey suit and pink tie, and at the square, determined character dressed in ugly woollen clothes who was his wife.

'Mr Donovan?' she asked, placing the shoe on the desk.

The man nodded. It was only then that she realized that desperation had made this man come here today. He was trembling and pale. She sat down opposite him and watched him sweat.

'Are you the person in charge of this case?' His voice squeaked with nervousness. She met his eyes and he flushed. 'Can I speak to a man officer?'

She leaned forward. 'No, Mr Donovan,' she said. 'No, you can't. I am in the middle of a murder investigation. A young woman's body was found raped and garrotted in the snow a week ago.' She slammed the shoe down on the desk. 'I think this was her shoe. I want to know how you acquired it. And I also want to know why you hung on to it when it is evidence.'

Donovan licked dry lips.

'Pictures of this shoe have appeared in all the major papers.' She watched him squirm. 'You take a paper?'

The hatchet-faced woman spoke, smoothing her billowing skirt towards her ankles. 'We do,' she said. 'He saw it.'

There was no empathy in her voice. She would not save his head from rolling.

Joanna paused, then nodded to Mike. 'Right,' she said. She flicked on the tape recorder.

'Mr Andrew Donovan, you are being questioned in connection with the rape and murder of Sharon Priest on the twenty-eighth of September nineteen ninety-six. You do not have to say anything. But it may harm your defence if you do not mention when questioned something which you may later rely on in court. Anything you do say may be given in evidence.' She gave Donovan a hard look. 'Understand?'

'Yes.'

'I am Detective Inspector Piercy. Also present is Detective Sergeant Korpanski. You wish to make a statement?'

Donovan looked around like a mouse when the trap snaps. 'Yes,' he said. 'I do.'

'You understand you have the right to have a solicitor present?'

Again he nodded. 'I don't want one. I just want my wife to hear everything I've got to say. The whole bloody lot,' he said desperately.

And that was what made Joanna suddenly turn her interest even more intensely on the man. Was he the one? She gave Mike a quick glance and saw he too was startled. Was this case about to be cracked by a confession from a quiet, seedy little man with cheap, flashy clothes and an over-dominant wife?

Mrs Donovan stood over her husband. 'Get on with it, Andrew,' she said, giving Joanna an angry glance. 'It seems my husband,' she said through clenched teeth, 'enjoys masturbating with a tart's shoe.'

'Be quiet, Mrs Donovan,' Joanna reacted angrily. 'Your husband is the one we want the statement from, please, not you.'

The woman folded her arms and glared at Joanna from her chair in the corner.

Joanna turned her attention to the man, who was

now fingering his collar as though he was about to choke.

'Where did you get the shoe from?' she asked.

He blinked. 'Last week,' he said timidly. 'It was a Wednesday.' He stopped and swallowed and Joanna considered offering him a glass of water. But she hardened her heart. Let him wait.

'It was the morning after the heavy snow,' he said. 'I had to cross the moors to Buxton. I had a meeting there.'

'Go on.'

Already she knew she was to be disappointed. This was to be no confession to major crimes but a sordid little story, of tacky habits and sexual perversion.

'At the top – near the farm – I got stuck in a drift.' He hesitated and risked a quick glance over his shoulder at his wife. 'I always take a shovel,' he said.

Mike couldn't risk a quick dig. 'Very wise, Mr Donovan,' he said.

'I was digging myself out, and I saw something in the snow.' Again he paused. 'Do you think I could have a drink of water?'

'In a minute,' Joanna said brusquely.

'I think the snowplough must have chucked it up,' he said. 'You know – it was sort of sticking half in the bank.'

'And?'

Donovan winced. 'I thought it was pretty.'

Behind him his wife gave a snort.

'I sort of . . . I put it in my car, took it home.'

'Why?'

He looked around the room and found Mike's eyes

– impassive. 'It reminded me of . . . pretty girls,' he said and stared at the floor.

'I see.' Joanna moved the shoe towards nim. Both were aware of the stains.

She met his eyes. 'Did you know,' Joanna asked quietly, 'that this shoe belonged to a girl who had been raped? Raped and then a wire cable pulled tight around her neck?'

Donovan licked his lips and nodded. 'Yes.'

'Did you see any sign of the girl?'

Donovan leaned across the interview table. 'I didn't see anything,' he said desperately. 'I was in a hurry. I was worried about getting through to Buxton.'

All four of them looked back at the shoe.

'Didn't you wonder at the time, Mr Donovan, how it had got there?'

'I thought her car must have got stuck – broken down.'

'Did you see a car?'

'No.'

'Did you see anything?'

'No . . . No, nothing. Only the shoe. That's all I saw.'

'Why didn't you bring it in when you'd seen the newspaper reports?'

'It wasn't going to help you,' he said desperately. 'It didn't have anything to tell you.'

'No? We would have liked to be the ones to judge that for ourselves,' Joanna said before adding softly, 'Why today, Mr Donovan?'

He looked startled. 'What do you mean? I've come forward, haven't I? No one forced me to come.' He looked at her with a touch of bravado. 'You didn't know

I had it. You'd never have known if I hadn't come forward.'

'No, we wouldn't have known. But Sharon Priest died a week ago today. We've had a lot of men searching everywhere for this shoe. It's been well publicized.' Again she asked the same question but this time a touch more aggressively. 'Why now, Mr Donovan? Why have you come here today?'

It was the wife who answered. 'Because I found him doing disgusting things with it. That's why. He only came here because of what I would think. I thought he might have killed her.' She looked at him with a fierce hatred. 'I thought he might be the one. The girl was raped, wasn't she?'

'Please, be quiet, Lizzie,' Donovan said. 'Sit down.'

Lizzie Donovan gaped at her husband. She flushed. An angry light appeared in her eyes. She pressed her lips together and sat back heavily in her chair.

Joanna stared at the small pale, man. 'And you weren't concerned about the shoe's owner?'

He blinked. 'At first,' he said. 'But I thought she must have got stuck and had managed to get free.' He stopped. 'All I knew was, she wasn't up there.' He looked at her. 'I called,' he said. And Joanna had a vivid picture of the man, holding the shoe, calling across the snowy expanse of moors.

She leaned forward. 'You were holding the shoe?'

'Yes.' He stared at her. 'It reminded me of Cinderella. The glass slipper.' His eyes rested on the shoe.

The letter that had tempted Sharon to meet her killer at the Quiet Woman had promised her Prince Charming.

Joanna looked again at Andrew Donovan. 'You knew Sharon Priest?'

He shook his head violently. 'No. I didn't know the girl.'

'She had a baby, supposedly by a married man, Mr Donovan.'

Lizzie Donovan was sitting on the edge of her seat, her head whipping from one to the other.

'Were you that married man, Mr Donovan?'

'No . . .' Again he shook his head. 'No. I never ever met her.'

Joanna glanced from the high-heeled black shoe with its diamanté buckle to Lizzie Donovan's podgy ankles spilling over their brown brogues. And in a flash she knew why the shoe had exerted such influence over Andrew Donovan.

He was looking defiantly at Joanna now. 'I knew she couldn't possibly have walked anywhere, not in these.' Again he stretched his finger and thumb to the height of the heel. 'And I wondered what sort of woman would wear this kind of shoe across the moors on a snowy night.'

'Whore!' spat Lizzie Donovan.

Mike spluttered. Joanna looked at him sharply.

It was strange how the shoe sat, high heeled and elegant, in the centre of the desk, dominating the whole interview almost haughtily.

'I just wondered . . .' he said apologetically.

His eyes were cold, with tiny, pin-pointed pupils. When he looked at her Joanna felt uneasy. She watched him.

Mike leaned right across the desk. 'Come on,

Donovan,' he said softly. 'You must have had some kind of a picture what she was like.'

Now Donovan looked rattled. He leaned back, away from Mike and blinked unhappily. 'No, sir,' he said. 'I didn't think.'

'I put it to you that you did,' Mike said. 'In fact I think you thought that the girl who wore these shoes was attractive.' He too put out a hand and touched the shoe, then stared hard at Donovan. 'In fact you fancied her so much you raped her then stuck the wire round her neck and twisted it. Didn't you?'

Now Donovan was terrified. 'I didn't,' he said. 'I didn't. I promise you.'

Lizzie Donovan was looking on pityingly without saying a word. She merely sat, watching impassively.

'Where were you on the Tuesday night that Sharon Priest was killed?' pressed Joanna.

Donovan stared at her.

'Mr Donovan,' she said. 'I really think you should acquire the services of a solicitor, don't you?'

The little man nodded.

'Will I be charged?'

'Yes. Charges relating to concealment of evidence and wasting police time,' she said. 'And we'll be testing samples from the dead girl's body to see whether they match up with your body samples.'

Donovan looked pleadingly at Joanna, but she met his eyes with frank dislike.

Joanna took Mike outside the interview room. 'Well?' she said. 'What do you think? Did he do it?'

Mike frowned. 'He could have. He was up there –
on the moors at some time. He could have been the
one who made the date.'

'You think she met Donovan that night at the Quiet
Woman?' She looked at him dubiously. 'And he kept
her shoe?'

He shrugged. 'I'm just saying it's a possibility,
Joanna.'

'And he was the one who killed Stacey?'

His dark eyes were appealing to her.

'I don't think it, somehow,' she said. 'I don't think
he's clever enough.' She stopped and frowned. 'He
doesn't fit my image of our killer. He seems –
pathetic . . . seedy. I can't picture him as a rapist. But
we'd better get his car in,' she said. 'He denies knowing
Sharon at all. Therefore there should be nothing of her
in that car. No hair . . . nothing. And let's get the shoe
down to the lab.'

She could not help the feeling of anti-climax.

'In the meantime, I suppose I'd better make that
visit to Randall Pelham.'

The solicitor lived in a smart, Edwardian detached
house on the Buxton road. Painted black and white
with a pretty verandah, it had an air of genteel
elegance.

She parked her car in the drive behind a black
Jaguar and knocked on the stout oak door.

Elspeth Pelham answered the door. She looked at
Joanna resignedly. 'Every time I see the police,' she
said, 'I have a feeling of déjà-vu, as though Deborah

only left yesterday.' The strain on her face was painful as she looked at Joanna. 'My husband,' she said with difficulty, 'believes she is alive, Inspector.' Her eyes looked haunted as she spoke. 'What woman would abandon a child?'

Joanna shifted uneasily.

'Sebastian is such a sweet little boy,' Elspeth Pelham continued, then she clutched at Joanna's arm. 'Deborah's dead, isn't she?'

Joanna touched the woman's shoulder. 'We think she might be,' she said.

Mrs Pelham's eyes filled with tears. 'Do you have children, Inspector?'

Joanna shook her head.

'Children are pain,' she said, 'with the tiniest amount of pleasure thrown in.' She turned round then and Joanna followed her into the house.

The hall was gloomy, panelled in some dark wood. A wide mahogany staircase led up and divided left and right in front of a beautiful stained-glass window depicting two sheep with a lamb.

Randall Pelham stood in the living-room doorway staring at her. He tightened his lips, stood back and the three of them entered the room.

The newspaper was casually dropped on the sofa, its headlines glaring: 'Police question man about Sharon killing.'

He turned to her. 'What do you have to tell me?'

She looked at him helplessly.

'Don't spare us,' he said. 'Please, Inspector . . . Nothing could be worse than not knowing.' He stopped.

'If our daughter is dead we would wish to give her a decent Christian burial. You understand?'

She nodded. 'I need to check some facts with you about the circumstances surrounding your daughter's disappearance,' she said. She paused. 'Anything I say to you is confidential – you understand?'

They both nodded. They were sitting together, on the sofa. An elderly couple whose one daughter had disappeared. And the tragedy clung around them like a fog.

Joanna pressed on. 'This girl – Sharon Priest. Have you ever heard her name before?'

They shook their heads.

'Your daughter never mentioned that name?'

Again a negative.

'The man who killed Sharon had killed another girl before – another young woman. She was from Macclesfield.'

The couple's eyes were fixed on her face.

'That was eighteen months ago,' she said, then paused again. 'Does the name Leanne Ferry mean anything to you?'

This brought recognition. 'She was a so-called friend of Deborah's,' Randall Pelham said gruffly. 'A feminist – a girl who made Deborah discontented.' Then he looked at Joanna shrewdly. 'What's the connection, Inspector?'

'She now lives with Sharon Priest's ex-boyfriend.'

Elspeth Pelham gave a tiny gasp. 'Oh.'

'These two facts make me a little uneasy about your daughter,' she said. 'Frankly, the police originally thought Deborah had walked out on her family – both you and her son.' She stopped. 'Obviously this puts things in a different light.'

The Pelhams were watching her as though hypnotized.

'Is there anything you feel you want to add?'

Still they sat, clutching each other's hands.

'Tell me about the day she disappeared.'

'She asked a friend, Sandy Beastall,' Elspeth told the story in a weary voice, 'to look after Sebastian. She said she was going shopping. She wanted some new clothes and some underwear. The people at the market saw her. She did buy some things. The friend was meant to be baby-minding anyway that evening, because Deborah had a date.'

Randall Pelham interrupted his wife. 'We don't know who the date was with and we never found out. Sandy said she was very excited. The last sighting was at three o'clock at the outdoor market. She was carrying some shopping bags.'

'Did anyone come forward to say they were supposed to be meeting Deborah that evening?'

'The police didn't really try too hard,' Randall Pelham said. 'Because she never went on that date, you see. The plan was that she went shopping, came home, got changed and went out. The fact that she disappeared in the middle of the day took the emphasis off the night-time date.'

Joanna nodded, then looked at Elspeth. 'You were close to your daughter?'

She nodded. 'I would have said so, yes,' she answered quietly. 'Perhaps a little less so when she returned from Saudi Arabia.' She stopped. 'Deborah seemed a little more hard-boiled after being there.'

'And that bloody spiky-haired female didn't help either.'

Joanna looked at Randall Pelham.

'Well – with her rights-for-women attitude and going on about men using women for their own ends. All that crap.'

The word was unexpected coming from him and Joanna smiled. 'Mr Pelham. I had the feeling that you suspected someone of being involved in your daughter's disappearance.' Joanna paused. 'Was it Leanne Ferry?'

He looked away. 'I had no proof.'

'But . . .'

'She had a lot of influence over Deborah,' he said fiercely. 'Deborah even began to talk like her.'

'Was there anything concrete we can go on?'

He shook his head.

Joanna was silent for a moment, digesting facts. But try as she might she couldn't see where Leanne Ferry fitted into the picture.

'Tell me . . . Do you really think Deborah is dead?' Elspeth Pelham asked again.

'It's possible,' Joanna said cautiously.

'By the same man?'

Joanna nodded.

'I see.'

'I've never understood,' Randall Pelham said slowly, 'why since that day we never heard anything. And neither has her ex-husband. Her son is now nearly three years old and has no recollection of his mother.'

Pelham was close to breaking down. He covered his face with his hand. His wife tightened her grip on him but he stood up. 'Where does Miss Ferry live now?'

'Please . . .' Joanna begged. 'Leave this to the police.'

Pelham gave her a sudden, malevolent look. 'I've done that for the last two years. Where has it got me?'

'Nowhere,' Joanna said calmly. 'But neither will harassing Leanne Ferry.'

Joanna left soon after that. The feeling of emptiness in the old house was painful, the couple's unhappiness tangible. She could hardly remember ever feeling more pity than she did for these two lonely, middle-aged people. And his social position and her bravery all added poignancy to the situation.

Chapter Thirteen

'Great morning for cycling, Joanna,' called Stuart as he came up level with her, and she nodded back in agreement, out of breath and apprehensive. She had seen another side to Stuart. A less attractive side.

'I'm still having trouble keeping up with you,' she panted.

But he took little notice and pedalled faster. 'You working this weekend?'

'Most of the time.'

He slowed down then and she caught up with him. 'Sure you won't spend an evening with me?' he urged. 'I know a great little restaurant.'

'I don't think so.'

He bent back down over his handlebars. 'Oh,' he said and quickened his pace.

She made a face, kept her head down and pedalled faster, swinging round the corner towards the hill. They were at the top before she caught him up again.

They cycled silently for half a mile before she turned to look at him. 'I don't know much about you, do I?'

He laughed it off. 'Not much to know. I work in the town.'

'What as?'

They were speeding along now. 'I trained as an engineer. As I said,' he laughed, 'I'm a nuts and bolts man.'

Her front wheel wobbled. 'Where exactly do you work?'

'Blyton's,' he said cheerfully.

She dropped right back then, feeling hollow. She and Mike had committed the cardinal sin of leaving someone out of the questioning, just because they hadn't been there at the time. There had been two engineers and they hadn't spoken to either of them.

Now she was curious about this one.

'You aren't married, are you, Stuart?'

He looked almost embarrassed. 'Course not. What do you take me for? I live with my mum.'

'No girlfriend?'

'Not at the moment.' Now he looked hurt.

'Why?'

'Nothing.'

She would prefer to interview both Stuart and the second engineer in a more formal atmosphere, and with Mike at her elbow.

She had never been so relieved to reach the turn-off and lift her hand to wave goodbye.

Stuart waved back and carried on and she watched him go with mixed feelings. She finished her journey in slow, thoughtful mode, and chained her bike to the railings.

The first person she spoke to was Mike. He was as mortified as she at their omission.

'OK,' he said, 'so we go back to Blyton's.'

'Exactly.'

The morning briefing was uneventful and she knew that without something positive to go on there was a danger of the officers becoming apathetic and bored with the case. After all, new crimes were being committed daily, many of which they would have a better chance of solving. And these days they were constantly being told how to measure their success – by convictions.

But this could be a dangerous period, when time could easily be wasted by lack of concentration. So Joanna planned to spend the morning concentrating on the positive aspects and specific tasks and attempting to raise morale. She made a quick decision.

'I think we should watch Christine Rattle. She's had a brick through her window. There's not much doubt it's Finnigan . . . the wording of the threat plus the phrase "stop rattling". Keep watching him, too – see what else he's getting up to . . . If any of you see him heading towards her, intercept him.' She stopped and glanced around the room. 'I don't trust him,' she said.

Timmis interrupted her. 'Why did Finnigan do it?' he said. 'He wasn't particularly prominent in our enquiries. All he's done is draw attention to himself. Why? Do you think there's something Christine Rattle isn't telling us?'

She gave a wry smile. 'There's always something they're not telling us, Timmis, don't you know that yet? They don't tell us for a variety of reasons. They're frightened, they don't understand the significance of what they know, or they're just plain stubborn. And, of course, someone isn't telling us all he knows because he is our bloody killer. And Christine Rattle might have taken it into her head to protect him. God knows why . . .' she muttered, and then felt unreasonably disloyal to Christine. She had until recently counted her as one of her friends . . . But sometimes the police could not afford the luxury of this most valued of life's commodities. She had learned that the hard way.

Timmis spoke up again. 'Do you think Finnigan's the killer, ma'am?'

She perched on the corner of the desk and crossed her legs.

'We don't know yet,' she said. 'We really don't know who our killer is. We're keeping open minds.' She made a face. 'You know how I hate guesswork and so-called hunches. I'm not in a desperate hurry. I simply want to get the right man to court. But I want to do that without further killings. We know Finnigan's a villain. We know he's violent, and he held a grudge against Sharon Priest. But the man we're looking for has raped and killed before. At least once.' She thought she might as well confide in them.

'We know that our killer was also responsible for Stacey Farmer's death in Macclesfield eighteen months ago. Well, some of you will remember the disappearance of a woman called Deborah Halliday, two years ago. Her body was never found, but I'm almost certain she's our third victim.' She glanced around the room, then added, 'And there's a link – Leanne Ferry, Deborah Halliday's best friend. Now living with Paul

Agnew, Sharon Priest's ex-boyfriend. DS Korpanski and I will be visiting her today.'

There was a muttering around the room.

Joanna turned back to the board. 'As for Finnigan, although we have no record of Finnigan ever having raped, we have to consider this. Would Sharon have left the pub with a man who had openly threatened her and beaten her up? Personally I don't think so. She was dressed for a date. The question is – with whom?'

Mike was chuntering. 'No evidence that Finnigan ever raped anyone? Your friend Ms Rattle is lying.'

'Well, we'll challenge Christine with that, but we can't force her to make a statement.'

'What about bringing Finnigan in?'

'It's worth a try,' she agreed.

Turning back to the room, she knew she was leaving the most important detail until last.

'Korpanski and I will also be visiting Blyton's later on to interview the two engineers who have so far escaped our attentions.'

Finnigan was surly and resentful at being hauled in. Accompanied by two uniformed officers, he sauntered through the office area, unshaven and reeking of stale sweat and lager and wearing a crumpled and stained T-shirt.

'What do you want me here for now?' he grumbled, then demanded legal aid.

Valuable time was wasted. It was an hour before an available solicitor arrived. He briefed Finnigan before turning to Joanna.

'Are you charging my client?'

Joanna shook her head. 'No,' she said smoothly. 'Of course not. But as well as the murder investigation we are also now investigating an unpleasant incident that took place the night before last.'

The solicitor opened his briefcase. 'And in connection with which investigation have you brought my client here today?'

'Both,' Joanna said.

'I was at home,' Finnigan said.

'You don't know at what time the offence was committed.'

'I was at home all night.'

Joanna leaned across the table. 'Witness intimidation carries a jail sentence these days,' she said softly.

'Bloody typical,' Finnigan looked aggrieved. The first sign of trouble and you come charging in on me. Well, you can't pin the killing on me,' he said. 'I never touched Sharon.'

'The night before last a brick was thrown through Christine Rattle's window. The brick was accompanied by a threatening note.'

Finnigan sniffed. 'Don't know nothing,' he said, folding his arms around his chest.

'Are you good at writing?' Joanna asked drily.

'Now what are you on about?'

The solicitor glanced again at his watch. 'Please, Inspector,' he said.

'Write "interfere".' She rolled a pencil across the interview table and pushed the pad across. 'No, better still, write this whole sentence down.'

Finnigan flushed.

'Bricks through windows, Mr Finnigan?'

'You can't prove a thing,' he muttered.

'Want to bet?'

The solicitor spoke. 'You don't have to say anything.'

Joanna wished the solicitor would shut up. She ignored him, but unfortunately Finnigan did not. He rolled the pencil back across the table.

'You haven't charged me.'

'Not yet, not yet.' She stood up. 'You can always live in hope, can't you?'

Finnigan eyed her, 'Prison?'

She nodded. 'As I said, witness intimidation does carry a prison sentence these days.'

Finnigan leaned back heavily in his seat. 'Look,' he said. 'I don't know about no bricks and things.' He gave an attempt at an ingratiating smile. 'But I think I can tell you something.'

'About Sharon?'

He nodded. 'I don't know if it's anything to do with her getting herself killed, but I think I know the married bloke she had the affair with. I know who Ryan's dad is.'

She could not suppress the feeling of elation.

Mike walked towards the table and bent over him. 'Who?'

'He drives a white Merc,' Finnigan said, avoiding looking at Mike. 'He goes into Blyton's but he doesn't work there. I can tell you the reg number of the car. It's personalized.'

Joanna already knew it. She made her hand into a

tight fist and looked down at it. Small facts, tiny pieces of a Chinese puzzle. The wooden sort that could never make a perfect sphere until you had each piece in exactly the right place. And this case was just beginning to take shape.

She nodded, then spoke to Finnigan again. 'What were you so afraid that Christine might "rattle" about, Mr Finnigan?'

Finnigan dropped his gaze but not before Joanna had read an uncertainty. The solicitor cleared his throat and for a moment the room was silent.

He was hiding something.

'It wouldn't be rape, would it?'

Finnigan's eyes bulged.

She glanced again at Mike, and let Finnigan go – for now.

It was time to turn her attentions to Leanne Ferry.

Paul Agnew lived in a small terraced house with bay windows and four black plastic dustbins standing in the garden. The street was ringing with the strains of pop music. The girl who answered his door was short and squat with bright, spiky hair. She wore wash-faded flowered leggings, a grubby pullover and a dour expression.

'Yeah?'

It wasn't hard to guess who she was.

'Leanne Ferry?'

The girl nodded.

Joanna showed her her card. 'I'm Detective Inspector Piercy and this is Detective Sergeant Korpanski.

We're investigating the rape and murder of Sharon Priest.'

'I didn't think you'd come here,' the girl said grudgingly but without a trace of apprehension. 'There's no point. Paul isn't in. He's at work. Anyway,' she added, 'you know everything. Paul finished with Sharon ages ago when she was expecting Ryan. He didn't even know she was in the pub that Tuesday. They had nothing more to do with each other. He couldn't stand her. And then he met me. And he didn't have no time for her any more. He didn't fancy her no more.'

'I haven't come to see Paul,' Joanna said. 'It's you I want to talk to.'

The girl's face twisted. 'Oh, charmed, I'm sure. You want to ask me about my boyfriend's ex?'

'No.' Joanna took a step forward. 'Leanne,' she said slowly. 'I think you can help us.'

'Help you what?' There was deep distrust in her voice.

'Can I come in?'

The girl looked around in a sudden, fleeting panic and Joanna read her mind.

'Look,' she said. 'I'm not on a hunt for grass. I don't care if you have a marijuana plantation in there. I'm not interested. We're talking about murder. Now, can I come in?'

Leanne stood her ground. 'No, you bloody can't. Not without a warrant. Not unless you tell me what you do want.'

Joanna took a deep breath. 'All right, then – on the doorstep where all your neighbours will hear.'

Leanne Ferry gave a chuckle. 'Listen, copper,' she said. 'Haven't you got no ears? Can't you hear all that music? They wouldn't hear anything if your beefy friend here was to rape and strangle me.'

Mike flushed and shifted uneasily. It was an unfortunate choice of words. The three of them were conscious of Sharon Priest's final struggle.

Leanne moved back, flat against the door, and without a word the two police filed past.

Leanne glanced up and down the street before closing the door and standing against it, her arms folded. The room was tiny, dark and claustrophobic.

'Go on, then,' she said.

And suddenly Joanna wasn't sure where to start. 'Tell me about Finnigan,' she began.

Leanne looked surprised. 'Finnigan? You want to know about Finnigan?'

'Yes.'

Leanne relaxed. 'He's a nothing,' she said. 'He's a violent, lager-drinking lout.'

Mike moved close to her. 'Is he a rapist?'

Leanne gave a shrug. 'It might just be a rumour. People say things. You don't always know they're true.'

'What things?'

And both police felt they already knew the rest. They had felt it instinctively in Finnigan's flat.

'Paul said . . .' Leanne swallowed, ' . . . Sharon told him Finnigan got a bit rough sometimes.'

'*How* rough?' Joanna demanded. '*How rough?*'

'Very.' Leanne was even more reluctant to say the next sentence. 'I think he tried something on with her friend Christine, too. He'd try it on with anybody.'

Joanna caught Mike's eye. They had never checked Finnigan's alibi but had let it ride because Sharon would never have left the pub with him. It was even more definite now. She had been wearing nothing but her best, new dress. Finnigan hadn't needed an alibi. In a way Sharon had been it.

'Anything else?'

'Sharon honestly thought he'd kill her,' she said. 'He seemed to really hate her after that night. She was really frightened of him.'

'So she left the trousers hanging out of the window?'

Leanne nodded. 'If it had been left to Sharon they'd still be there now.'

'But they're not.'

Leanne seemed frozen, almost stuck to the door. Very slowly she moved away and headed towards the narrow staircase. Halfway up she stopped and looked down on them. 'I've got them,' she said, before covering the last few steps to the top.

Neither Mike nor Joanna spoke until she reappeared holding a pair of black jogging pants.

She gave an abrupt laugh. 'Paul sort of inherited them,' she said, 'when he met Sharon. Hanging out of the window, they still were – but he wasn't frightened of Finnigan. They were upsetting her so he got them down. They're nice trousers.' She handed them to Joanna.

Somehow she had imagined that the word 'trousers' related to a creased, formal garment. Neither had visualized casual wear but, holding them, Joanna realized that to Christine, Finnigan, Agnew and the rest, jobless and permanently skint, this was a pair of trousers, black jogging pants, sportswear, cycling trousers.

Her eyes were on Mike as she spoke. 'We'd better get across to Blyton's straight away.'

Chapter Fourteen

It was still only early afternoon but it was dull and grey. The threat of further snow hadn't quite receded. The lights were already on at Blyton's, pale spots winking through the gloom, and as Joanna and Mike drew up they could hear the clank of machinery.

During the journey she had filled him in on some of the details, but there were more – many more – that she hadn't told him and she knew she never would.

The secretary met them at the main door, her pale eyes bright with curiosity and suspicion.

But Joanna was being careful. She had learned before not to cast blame until she was 100 per cent sure. There was still room for doubt.

In spite of the plaque with Stuart Thorr's name on the door she didn't at first recognize him. Out of his cycling shorts, helmet and Oakleys and in his dark suit, plain tie and white shirt he looked completely different . . . more ordinary, shorter, less muscular, his face a little plumper.

She recalled a caption from a magazine, 'Cyclists are sexy'. On their bikes, maybe, she reflected grimly. Off them, you might not recognize them.

This wasn't the Stuart she knew. And it seemed he had the same difficulty.

'Joanna?' he said, frowning. '*Joanna?*' Then he stood up, half smiling, disbelieving but still welcoming. 'What on earth are you doing here?' The smile lasted until he caught sight of Mike. 'Who are *you?*'

To cover both anger and embarrassment, Joanna took refuge in formality. 'Detective Inspector Piercy,' she said, 'and this is Detective Sergeant Korpanski.'

Stuart remained silent.

'I believe you knew a woman called Sharon Priest.'

At the station Stuart refused a solicitor and sat opposite Joanna across the interview table, his eyes fixed on her face as though he trusted her. She found his whole demeanour puzzling. Surely he could not be relying on her to get him off? It didn't make sense. He must see what a poor position he was in.

She pressed the record button on the tape machine and read out the date, the time, the officers present.

'You answered an advert in the personal column of the *Evening Standard*?'

Stuart nodded.

Mike had to remind him to speak. The result was a quiet 'Yes.'

'You exchanged letters?'

'Yes.' He smiled. 'And all the time she didn't have a clue it was me.'

'And eventually you arranged to meet?'

'Yes.'

'On the twenty-seventh of September you met at the Quiet Woman public house?'

Another quiet 'Yes,' and Joanna moved her hand towards her face. This was all going a little too well. He was too comfortable and his expression was still too trusting.

'Stuart,' she said, 'are you sure you wouldn't like a solicitor present?'

He looked almost amused. 'No,' he said. 'There's no need for that – really. No need.'

'So you met Sharon at the pub.'

'Yes.'

'Then what?'

He gave a secretive smile. 'I'd planned to . . .'

Joanna hardly dared breathe.

Stuart looked up, innocent-eyed. 'I'd planned to take her home to meet my mother,' he said, oblivious to the effect he was having on the two police officers present.

'She's a remarkable woman. I think she and Sharon would have had a great deal in common.' He smiled. 'You see, both were single parents. Sharon was having a struggle bringing up her three on her own and my mum had been through exactly the same with me.' Again he gave that strange smile. 'My mother would have helped her.'

'So you took her back?'

'No. She wasn't at all interested in meeting my mum.' He sounded puzzled. 'In fact . . .' His voice was growing angry now. 'She didn't seem pleased that it was me at all. She looked quite put out. I'd thought . . . after all . . .'

He leaned forward, forearms on the table, confiding now. 'I was really the one who broke up her marriage. If it hadn't been for me . . .'

Mike spoke brusquely. 'Getting caught with your trousers down?'

Stuart flushed.

Joanna shook her head very slowly and, switching off the tape recorder, she motioned Mike outside.

'He's a nutcase.'

'A guilty nutcase?'

'He doesn't seem to realize what sort of position he's in.'

She peered in through the window of the interview room. Stuart was leaning back in his chair, his hands, relaxed, on his lap. There was not a trace of tension about him.

Alan King wafted past and handed her a report. It took one minute to digest the information and repeat it to Mike.

'The shoe showed up plenty of semen. But the semen was different from the samples taken from the murdered women. Not surprisingly Andrew Donovan is off the hook.'

Mike's answer was to jerk his thumb towards the door. 'But he's not.'

It was their cue to resume questioning.

'OK, Stuart,' she said. 'So you met Sharon at the Quiet Woman and took her off to meet your mother.'

'I would have done,' he said comfortably, 'but she got really angry about the idea. She started shouting at me, said I had a mother complex.' There was a quick flash of teeth before he closed his mouth. 'I haven't,' he said. 'She was quite wrong. I only thought . . .'

'So you got angry with her.' Mike's voice was brutal. 'You raped and strangled her, then dumped her body on the moor.'

'No, I didn't,' he said, eyes wide open. 'She told me to let her out of the car. It was a cold night, and she was only wearing a thin dress. I offered to drive her back to the Quiet Woman but she didn't seem to want that. The last I saw of her she was walking back to town.'

Chapter Fifteen

It was only to Mike that she could bear to voice her doubts. 'He could be telling the truth.'

He stared at her. 'You must be joking.'

'But what if it is the truth?' she insisted. 'What if he really did drop her off and someone else saw her walking, through the snow, wearing nothing but a thin dress?'

'Joanna.' He was staring at her as though she was mad, but she persisted.

'What if Thorr is telling the truth?' He had stopped being Stuart from the moment she had realized he was a chief suspect.

'Impossible.'

'*Improbable*,' she corrected.

'Far too much of a coincidence. Besides,' he said. 'Who else?'

'Well, it seems to me fairly important we get that question answered without a shadow of a doubt. I thought we might visit Haworth.'

Mike just stared.

'We've charged Thorr, got him in custody,' she said firmly. 'If he is guilty we have nothing to lose. We know Haworth was out the night Sharon died so let's

227

go and see what he's got to say. We needn't tell him we've already got a suspect.' She wagged her finger at the burly Detective Sergeant. 'Don't think we've got all the answers yet, Mike. We haven't.'

Haworth was furious. She could hear him remonstrating through the thin walls of his office . . . Police intimidation . . . harassment . . .

Not yet, she thought.

He glared at them as they entered his office.

'Good morning, Mr Haworth,' she said pleasantly. 'I'm sorry to have to come and see you again. There are just one or two little problems, you see, with your statement.'

'What problems?'

Joanna sat down and crossed her legs. 'Oh, nothing we can't smooth out, I'm sure.'

'Inspector,' he said with a scowl, 'was it really necessary to come here to my office and disrupt my working day? If there were questions you wanted answering surely you could have contacted me by telephone?'

'We've wasted enough time already, Mr Haworth. We're anxious to get this case sewn up.'

Mike shuffled behind her, as Joanna spread her hands out on the desk. 'I want to ask you again about the night Sharon Priest died.'

'For goodness' sake,' the accountant said brusquely. 'I already told you all this. I was at home watching television, with my wife.'

'And your car?'

'In the drive.' He was close to exasperation.

Joanna nodded. 'I see,' she said. 'And you didn't go out?'

'How many times do . . .?'

She leaned across the desk. 'You didn't go out – not at all – you're sure?'

And then the penny dropped. Something in the man's face changed. He looked a little less angry, a little more nervous. He narrowed his eyes and spoke slowly.

'What exactly are you getting at?'

Mike stepped forward. 'We have a witness who says your car was seen on the Buxton road, heading down from the moors at about two o'clock in the morning.'

Haworth glared at him. 'The witness is lying,' he said. 'Or mistaken.'

'I don't think so,' Joanna said quietly.

The accountant shrugged. 'Well, who is this witness? Is it someone reliable?'

Joanna stared hard into his face. '*I* saw you, Mr Haworth. You overtook me at great speed.' She paused. 'Now, where had you been?'

For a moment the accountant seemed unable to speak. He was breathing hard and his face was pale. When he spoke he sounded dazed. 'You saw me?'

'Yes,' Joanna said. 'Quite a coincidence, isn't it?'

Dumbly he nodded.

'Come on, Haworth,' Mike was getting irritated. 'Stop telling little stories and give us the truth. Where had you been?'

Joanna made a swift decision. She would not tell Haworth she had noted that there was no snow on the roof of his car. Instead she would let him stew – believe they thought he was the killer while she watched him carefully.

'You see, Mr Haworth,' she said pleasantly, 'we have a couple of problems. Sharon Priest was murdered that night. And you – for some reason – decided to lie to us and pretend you had been in all evening. Detective Sergeant Korpanski and I both know that you did, in fact, go out – quite late. Unfortunately, being in the police force, we are bound to ask ourselves, Why is he lying? What is he hiding? And, finally, What other lies has he told us?' She gave him a deceptively friendly smile. 'I'm sure you can understand our dilemma, Mr Haworth.'

He licked dry lips.

'So let's start with where you'd been that night.'

'Just for a drive.' Haworth swallowed.

'On the moors?'

'No.' He paused, his eyes darting from one to the other. 'I was thinking of going up there – just for some peace – time to think, but it was too snowy. I was worried about getting stuck.'

'Well now.' Korpanski was pressing home his advantage. 'Inspector Piercy and I have been wondering about another lie you told us – whether you knew Sharon Priest a bit better than you let us believe.'

Haworth swivelled round in his chair and looked carefully past the burly detective at the white walls of his office. Then slowly he nodded.

'I think it's time you consulted a solicitor,' Joanna said.

*

Haworth's solicitor was a smart, trim woman in her forties wearing a businesslike grey suit and little make-up apart from scarlet lipstick, which she licked from time to time as though it had a flavour of its own.

It was she who spoke first. 'My client is prepared to volunteer certain information,' she said, 'of his own free will, in the hope that it will prove of some assistance in catching the killer of Ms Priest.'

They were back at the station, in a stuffy interview room. Haworth was tugging at his tie as though it was strangling him.

'So, Mr Haworth?'

'I did know Sharon,' he admitted. 'I gave her a lift home one day from Blyton's.' He gave an attempt at a smile. 'It was pouring with rain. She didn't even have a mac.'

His words conjured up the image Joanna had been forming of a young woman dressed in a thin dress and high heels struggling through the snow. She gave Haworth a sharp look. It was another small part of the picture.

'It was a long time ago,' he said. 'I dropped her off at her council house because I didn't want her to get wet. After that, I frequently took her home. Once or twice I went in and had a drink.'

Without looking at Mike, Joanna knew he would be rolling his eyes. There was no point beating about the bush. 'You became lovers, Mr Haworth,' Joanna said bluntly.

'It wasn't quite like that,' he said stiffly.

'So what was it like?' Mike was sounding rude but Joanna was past caring.

231

'My wife and I, as I told you, have no children.' He cleared his throat. 'In fact we are unable to have children.' The tiny muscle at the corner of his mouth was twitching. 'And this is a matter of grief to us both.'

His solicitor gave him an encouraging smile.

'One night when I spoke to Sharon she told me what a curse both her kids were to her. I found it rather ...' He winced, searching for the word, ' ... unfair.'

'So you made an arrangement that she should bear you a child.'

'She offered,' he said. 'I didn't ask her. I wouldn't have done that. It was she who pointed out that she bore children easily and suggested she should have one for us. We were not short of money. She was. It would be a financial transaction.'

'Which didn't work, did it? Because when it was time for her to hand over the child she refused.'

Haworth was looking increasingly strained. 'That's right,' he said quietly. 'She said she loved him too much to hand him over.'

Mike spoke then. 'That must have made you extremely angry.'

'Yes.' Too late he realized what he had said. 'I mean, no. Not that angry. I – understood. I helped her, gave her money. After all, the child was my son.'

'But when you saw her walking along the road, back towards the town, you picked her up?'

'I admit I was out that night, just driving, but I didn't see her. If I had I would have given her a lift certainly. It was a cold night.'

'And yet again she was inadequately dressed.'

But Haworth was too sharp to fall into that trap. 'As I didn't see her,' he said, 'I really can't tell you what she was wearing.'

Joanna played her trump card then, turning to the solicitor. 'Tell me,' she said. 'Mr Haworth is Ryan's father. Presumably this could be proved by DNA testing?'

The solicitor nodded, flicking a glance at Haworth.

'And if it was proved by DNA testing I assume he would have legal rights over the child in preference to anyone else?'

The solicitor nodded again.

'I thought so.'

Haworth was blustering. 'It's no motive for murder. Surely you wouldn't think I'd kill her to get at my son? I'd be in prison.'

'If you were found out.'

Chapter Sixteen

It was past eleven by the time she arrived back at the cottage, but then she was lucky to get home at all. Neither Thorr nor Haworth would see their own beds that night. Even as she put her key in the door the telephone was ringing. Wearily she picked it up. It was Matthew and he sounded upset.

'Please, Jo,' he said, 'can I come round to the cottage tonight?'

He knocked on her door five minutes later.

'I thought you were away for a few days, on your conference.' She studied his face. 'Blackpool, wasn't it?'

He nodded, gave a feeble attempt at a grin. 'Joanna,' he said.

She moved towards him, let her head drop against his shoulder.

'Joanna,' he said again, brushing her hair with his lips. Then he tilted her chin upwards.

It was much more than a hungry kiss. As his arms tightened around her she could feel his heart beating, his chest movement with each breath, the heat from his body. But it was the violence of her own reaction that shocked her as she clung to him.

'Joanna,' he was murmuring and she looked again at his face. His troubled eyes looked bark brown. And she knew that something was very wrong.

'What is it, Matthew?' she demanded, pulling away from him.

He was still watching her with that hungry, desperate look, frowning and breathing hard as though he had been running.

'Are you going to tell me or do I have to guess?'

He let her go and led her to the sofa, still gripping her hand.

'I was fool enough to think I had everything worked out,' he said quietly. 'I moved out of the farmhouse. I thought Jane would be able to sell it eventually.' He smiled. 'I found myself somewhere to live. I took out a short lease on a flat. Plenty of time, I thought, for us to work out what we really wanted.'

He looked at her with anguish in his face. 'Can you explain why,' he said, 'if four out of ten marriages end in divorce why the hell *I* can't seem to manage it?'

'Matthew,' she said, pulling her hand away, 'are you going to explain what you're talking about?'

'Eloïse is in hospital,' he said. 'The little tiger is starving herself until Daddy comes home.'

Joanna nodded.

'The little tiger,' he said with a touch of pride, 'is currently being drip-fed in the paediatric ward of the hospital. She insists she's on a hunger strike.'

Joanna felt hatred for the child searing through

her, hot and furious. She stood up. 'You've come to the wrong place for medical advice, Matthew.'

He stood too, taller than she, eyes blazing.

'We're talking about my daughter here,' he said. 'My daughter's life.'

Joanna was shaking with rage. 'Then go home,' she said. 'But don't involve me.' Her fury made her incautious. 'And if you want to know how other people can manage to divorce, I'll tell you. Because you, Matthew, may be sexy and intelligent and, yes, very good looking. But you're weak. Your wife is icy, cruel, selfish and unstable. However, she has an iron will and she has no intention of letting you go – ever. And as for your daughter . . .' She took two steps forward. 'Eloïse is a monster.'

For the rest of her life she would remember the shock on Matthew Levin's face.

With a shaking hand he put his glass down on the table and without looking at her he walked out.

She stood for a moment staring after him, then she opened a drawer in the table, found a cigarette. And for the first time in eight years she set a match to it.

Chapter Seventeen

She didn't sleep at all that night but lay anxiously tossing and turning.

For the first few hours all her turmoil was provoked by Matthew. She had always been so sure he loved her, right from their first, frenzied lovemaking. Even now she didn't doubt it, but she hadn't realized his love for Eloïse was stronger. Stupidly she had concentrated on his wife while discounting his daughter, but it was the daughter who would prove the insurmountable obstacle, not Jane.

But if the first half of the night was occupied by visions of Matthew, during the second half he was replaced by Sharon Priest.

Images wandered in and out of her mind. It was only now that she was realizing what a complex character Sharon had been, bent on survival, on having a good time yet struggling with her three children, using anything to earn money, by cleaning and, now, surrogacy.

She had been both streetwise and naive, clever and yet stupid, used and yet manipulative. She had written the advert, that pathetic, silly attempt to find happiness, excitement, romance and sparkle. An attempt to realize illusions.

Prince Charming had answered.

Stuart.

The whole thing would have been funny – Stuart turning up as the man of her dreams, only for her to find she'd already had an affair with him. That image was replaced by the black high heels, glass slippers, Sharon, shivering at the pub, not wanting to wear a coat that clashed with her best dress. But unable to afford anything more suitable.

So she had shivered. Sharon must have been excited as she waited in the pub. And then who had turned up? Someone she must secretly have laughed about. The trousers left hanging out of the window seemed so ridiculous. Passers-by must have seen them and laughed. Finnigan had known how to parade his wife's infidelity. And any romantic illusions Sharon might have nursed must quickly have been dispelled by the trousers, waving half-mast.

After her initial fear of Finnigan had evaporated how she must have laughed at the memory of Stuart pedalling furiously away from the scene. Even Joanna could laugh at the thought of a naked man on a bicycle. Cyclists are sexy?

So when Stuart had turned up at the Quiet Woman that night Sharon must have been disappointed. Weeks of build-up for nothing.

Instead of the Don Juan, Don Quixote had turned up, yet, according to the barmaid, she had gone willingly.

Joanna shivered. It was in these dark, quiet

moments that the brutality of rape and murder hit home. It had been an ugly way to die. Ugly and brutal.

Joanna got up then, with the feeling that these last few thoughts had contained the answer.

She would not sleep again until the killer was identified, so she threw on a towelling robe and padded downstairs to make coffee and switch on the central heating.

Reluctantly she pulled her little-used Peugeot 205 out of the garage and drove to the station.

The desk officer watched her walk in sympathetically.

'No sleep, Inspector Piercy?'

Almost in a dream, she shook her head and asked him to give Korpanski an early call.

He arrived half an hour later, puffy-eyed and cross. To compensate for the unearthly hour she went to the coffee machine.

'OK,' he yawned. 'What is it?'

'I think we can work it out,' she said.

He was still yawning and downing the coffee. 'Come on, then, share the good news. And by the way, how are the prisoners this morning?'

'About to go home.'

He sat up. 'What? Both of them?'

She nodded.

He took a deep gulp of coffee. 'Go on, I can tell you're dying to say something.'

Her hand was on the scattered letters. 'We've never checked out Finnigan's alibi, have we?'

'We didn't need to. She wouldn't have got in the car with him.'

'She might have if she was cold.'

She waited for Mike to absorb this last sentence before ploughing on. 'We're all agreed it was a vicious, brutal crime. And we know he is a brutal, vicious man with a hatred for women. We also know he is a rapist, although no charges have ever been brought.'

Mike looked troubled. 'We don't know he's a murderer, Joanna.'

'He's more likely than the other two we've had banged up overnight.'

'What about the Macclesfield girl?'

'He really did answer her advert,' she said. 'But it was Stuart Thorr who answered Sharon's. The answer's here, Mike. The letters were written by two different people. Finnigan's are blunt, obvious, misspelt. Stuart's were – well, let's just say they were two opposite personalities. Stacey was murdered by the man she had gone out with that night, but Sharon's date turned out be someone she found almost ridiculous – Thorr. Reluctantly she goes along with him, disappointed, but halfway to his house he makes a suggestion which she finds so crazy she actually gets out of the car and starts to walk back to Leek. But it's snowing and she's wearing the thinnest of dresses. So when Finnigan happens along, although she knows from experience that he's dangerous, she gets in the car with him. It's the last choice she is able to make and it's the wrong one. It was the very chance he'd hoped for, the one woman he hated most. He rapes and garrots her before dumping her body up on the moor.'

'Proof?' Mike asked.

'Eventually, a blood sample,' she said. 'But before that we can look over his flat.'

Finnigan was lying on his back snoring when they broke down the door. Joanna took fiendish delight in shaking him awake and cautioning him while he complained he had a full bladder. She was only sorry the caution wasn't longer.

The SOCOs had a field day. Newspaper clippings, practically the entire personal column, some with rings around, some, ominously, with red ticks and underlinings . . . But it was in the car that they found the more specific evidence, Sharon's hair, a few thin, red threads, some minute traces of blood. And neatly stacked in the boot under the spare wheel, almost like firewood, were pieces of broom handle, sawn into lengths roughly a foot long, together with some coils of cycle brake cable wire. Joanna counted them. There were eight. She had never felt more relieved to catch a killer and as she watched the police surgeon draw a syringe full of blood from Finnigan's arm she felt sudden elation. Not for the world would she do any other job.

Chapter Eighteen

Leaving Stuart to Mike's tender mercies, she derived some pleasure from being the one to release Haworth. Looking a bit more dishevelled than he had the night before, he needed a shave and his teeth cleaning. He slumped in the chair and scowled at her.

'Good morning,' she said brightly. 'I'm delighted to inform you that you're free to go.'

He stared at her, then rasped his hands over his chin. 'You have a suspect?'

Joanna nodded. It was the first time it had hit her that there must have been a relationship between Sharon Priest and Haworth. Maybe he had even been fond of her.

'Inspector,' he said. 'I want you to know I am sorry about what happened to Sharon. But the fact remains that I am the little boy's father. I am prepared to take a blood test to prove the point and my wife and I want custody. And by the way, Inspector.' Some of the old haughtiness was creeping back into Haworth's voice. 'Perhaps you'll tell Mrs Priest that there is a law against trying to obtain money by extortion.' The news didn't surprise her. Doreen had some of her daughter's talent for irregular ways of making money.

'Do you want to press charges?'

'I want her to leave me alone,' he said, 'and stop spreading gossip.'

'Will you tell him?' she asked curiously.

'You mean about his parentage?' Haworth stared ahead. 'To be honest, I don't know. We might say he was adopted and leave out the details, but it would mean moving away from this town. People here have very long memories.'

It was a phrase Colclough repeated when she was summoned to his office half an hour later.

He began with the case and a scrutiny of the prosecuting evidence, and she could tell from the happy wobble of his jowl that he was content. 'Has he confessed to both murders?'

She shook her head. 'He's confessed to nothing. Not Stacey Farmer, not Sharon Priest and not Deborah Pelham either.'

'You're still convinced she's one of his victims?'

'I'm not *sure*, sir.'

He nodded. Then his face changed as he moved on to her personal life.

'I've mentioned this before, Piercy,' he said. 'Keep your nose clean. However, in this particular instance I can't see you're to blame. I have been in contact with Mrs Levin and pointed out the areas of the law which she could be contravening.'

He looked up. 'That's all, Piercy, for now.'

She left feeling furious with him for the paternalistic, interfering attitude and yet, like a domineering, bossy father, maybe, just maybe, he had her best interests at heart.

It was the next day and Joanna was sitting in the office, working with Mike, when the door opened. She looked up. A thin young woman, dressed in faded jeans, was staring at her.

For a few seconds the room was silent.

Even Mike said nothing. It was as though all three were dumb. And Joanna did not want to be the one to break the silence.

Finally the girl spoke in a cracked, hard voice. 'Which one of you's Piercy?' she asked.

Joanna blinked. 'Me,' she said quietly and the girl sank down on to one of the chairs.

'You've been looking for me.'

'I have?'

The girl nodded.

It was Mike who recovered first. 'Well, who the hell are you, love?' he asked.

The girl swivelled round in her chair, shaking her head. 'Don't you recognize me?'

They stared at her, then shook their heads.

'The so-called good-time girl?' She sounded angry. 'You've been hanging around my dad . . . pretending to know something about me.'

And then the penny dropped.

'Where have you been?' Joanna said softly.

The girl dropped her face into her hands. 'To hell,' she said. 'To hell.'

'You left your son?'

'I had to,' the girl said fiercely. 'Don't you see? I was a rotten mum. It was better for him that I left him. And the longer I'd left him the harder it would be to ever return. Sebastian wouldn't know me,' she said.

'And for you, Deborah? What's best for you?'

The girl's tears were flowing freely now.

Mike was scowling. 'Well, where have you been?' he demanded. 'What have you been doing? How have you lived?'

Deborah Pelham turned to face him. 'You wouldn't believe me,' she said.

'Try me.'

But she gave a cynical shrug and turned her attention back to Joanna. 'Well, I'm back now,' she said. 'So you can call off your bloodhounds.'

And Joanna found that she didn't want the answer to any of Mike's questions. She met Deborah Pelham's eyes and nodded. 'Your father will be pleased to see you,' she said.

Deborah Pelham gave an ugly laugh. 'You really think so?' she said. 'He that was lost is found?' She glared at Joanna. 'You think he'll kill the fatted calf? No way,' she said. 'No way.' Her face looked old, ugly and twisted.

'He wanted to bury me,' she said. 'He wanted you to find my body, not some tired old whore who abandoned her son. Understand? I will be nothing but an embarrassment to him.'

She stood up stiffly, turned and walked out of the room.

*

Four days later Finnigan was finally charged with the two murders.

On the following day Joanna was sitting in her office with Mike, trying to anticipate the defence so that they could safely lob the anticipated manslaughter plea straight out of the window, together with the plea of insanity.

'It'll be a case of diminished responsibility,' Mike was arguing.

'No chance.'

'Keep your hair on, Joanna,' he said. 'I was only saying what the plea will be.'

'I'll work to convince the CPS,' she said. 'Finnigan was sane when he killed. A cold, calculating killer without pity for his victims who would have carried on and on until he was stopped.' The chilling vision of the neat pile of sawn-up broomsticks remained imprinted on her mind, each one representing another victim, another police investigation, another cluster of grieving relatives.

Mike was rolling a pencil between his fingers. 'I'll tell you something that puzzles me, Jo.'

'What?'

'She was disappointed when she saw it was Thorr who had turned up. Who do you think she hoped it would be?'

'I think Haworth,' she said decisively. 'He must have seemed personable to her, polite, wealthy. Compared with Finnigan and Agnew, he must have seemed wonderful.'

He gave her a sideways glance. 'And what about Thorr?'

She flushed.

Mike was laughing at her.

She couldn't resist a telephone call to the children's ward to ask how Eloïse Levin was. A bright, cheery nurse answered. 'Eloïse? Oh, she's fine. Her father's with her at the moment. She'll probably go home later on today.' There was a pause before she asked, 'Who shall I say phoned?'

Joanna was stuck, but the nurse supplied the answer. 'I'll just say a friend,' she said.

Joanna replaced the receiver.

Chapter Nineteen

It was four weeks later on a golden day, almost at the end of October, and Joanna was laying the circlet of flowers on the mound of earth, still unmarked by a headstone.

She didn't hear the woman approach but when she looked up she saw Doreen Priest, holding October and William by the hand.

'What are you doing here?' Mrs Priest demanded. 'She wasn't your friend. She wasn't your sister. You didn't even know her. She was just another murder victim to you.'

Joanna opened her mouth to speak. But she couldn't find the right words. There wasn't a platitude that existed to fill the silence. Even the two children were quiet, watching her through round eyes, their hands clutching their grandmother's.

Doreen Priest flicked the wreath aside contemptuously and replaced it with a small bunch, tied with pink florist's ribbon.

'There's your mother,' she said to the children. 'She's under there. So there's no use you keep askin' for her. She's gone. She won't be back. There's no use your cryin' for her. Understand?'

The two children nodded.

She gave Joanna a hard look. '*He*'s had Ryan,' she said. 'He were 'is dad anyhow. I'll mind these two. They've no real dad. I'll bring them up,' she said. 'So no harm's done.'

> '*And will your mourn your sister?*
> *Will you lay a wreath on her grave?*'

No, Joanna thought. The answer was an emphatic no. She would not mourn but continue with her own life and her own work.

So she left the graveyard and drove back to the station. For now there was work to be done.